I0666349

The Space Adventure of Alex

First Edition

Published by The Nazca Plains Corporation
Las Vegas, Nevada
2009

ISBN: 978-1-934625-96-5

Published by

The Nazca Plains Corporation ®
4640 Paradise Rd, Suite 141
Las Vegas NV 89109-8000

PUBLISHER'S NOTE
The Space Adventure of Alex is a work of fiction created wholly by *Ainsley's* imagination. All characters are fictional and any resemblance to any persons living or deceased is purely by accident. No portion of this book reflects any real person or events.

Model Photo, Niko Guido
Cover, Blake Stephens
Art Director, Blake Stephens

Dedication

This book is lovingly dedicated to Ronnie.
My true love, my Joel. May he rest in peace.

The Space Adventure of Alex

First Edition

Ainsley

Introduction

The year is 2523 and mankind has long ago conquered most disease, government corruption and hunger in the world. Man has now ventured out into space and settled on the moon, Mars and Ganymede, a moon of Jupiter. Man has also reached some of the nearer stars. The one problem mankind has not conquered is the dilemma of sex and love. Alex, as a man attracted sexually to other men, is protected under the 29th amendment to the US Constitution. However, he is still reluctant to declare his sexual status or preference. He attended the space academy on earth and joined the Space Corps. He takes his first assignment on a very large space ship making the milk run between the near planets and moons that are habitable close to the earth. He wants to train to go to the stars now that mankind has a faster than light drive. These star drives actually allow travel in an alternate medium. The Universe is now potentially man's domain. However, on his way to the stars, Alex wrestles with the age old problems of an active sex life. He meets several interesting people and has an abundance of fun sexually. Alex is very content with his life. However, he finally realizes something is missing in his life despite his very active sexual affairs.

Alex travels in a ship that has a complement of 1800 corps members transporting cargo and passengers to the off world colonies. Alex has received several proposals of marriage from his sexual friends, but does not want to commit himself to one man. This is Alex's story of his adventures in space and his sex escapades as he begins his journey into the rest of his life and into space. A journey into two arenas that are both about as big and both with unlimited potentials. They are not, however, without their own dilemmas. While the work is entirely fictional, the problems Alex faces are real. They are some of the same problems we all face today. The solutions he discovers may only work for Alex and not for you. It is hoped that his adventures well stimulate both your mind and your body.

Chapter One

My name is Alexander Peter Beauregard Franklin Carpenter, VII, and I hate my name. I think my father hated his name also, but because the family always passed on a good part of its wealth to the next generation, I kept the name and took their money. A good portion of their money is now my money. It may be tied up in a trust until I reach 50 standard earth years old, but that is perfectly all right with me. The name Alexander was from Alexander the Great. A famous General who conquered most of the know world thousands of years ago. No, he was not a relative. Peter was from Peter the Great some guy in Russia. No, he wasn't a relative either. Franklin, after Franklin Delano Roosevelt, an old American President. I think he was someone who wasn't afraid of anything or something like that. He had some saying about not fearing anything. No, he wasn't a relative either. Now you get the idea about our family. We want to look big and impressive, but we're not, or at least I don't think we are. I think Beauregard was actually my grandfather's brother's name. But, I never knew him and I don't believe a word of all this bullshit that people have told me about all these people. I call myself Alex, because we didn't have any Alex in my school, and I don't know any, and I liked the nickname. I didn't want to be mixed up with anyone else. My mother always called me son or dear, and my father called me Beau.

I got alone fine with my parents and they really loved me and were good to me. I have no complaints, but I also didn't have much of a childhood. My mother had her charity work, so I had a governess to help raise me when mother was busy most of the day. I was an only child. My mother said she couldn't have any more children, but I think it was because she didn't like the idea of being stretched out of shape by a baby. I know that dad would have thought it was a waste of good money to pay a surrogate to incubate a baby. And probably knowing dad, he would not opt for artificial insemination, he would have picked the surrogate and planted the seed himself. Not that he didn't love mom, but he was a typical man. Take every advantage of every situation you can. I think he appreciated the ladies. I think that once I was born, a male to carry on the family name, he was content to be married to mother, whom I know he loved very much. He probably got his sexual pleasure with her without having to pay for another child. Most families can petition for authorization to have a second and sometimes a third child, and it will be granted especially if they have the money to support the child. However, they chose not to do so. They were putting all their eggs in one basket, me. Many marriages are compromises of the strangest sorts. Who am I to criticize? They actually loved each other and that was good enough for me at that age.

Our family lives a long time, and while the average life span of an earth normal person is around 150 earth standard years, we usually live to the ripe old age of at least 175. Two of my great, great grandparents lived to about 200 earth standard years. I know you are impressed, since anything over about 140 is more than you're are promised by medical science barring accidents or being shot in the bed of another man's wife or girlfriend. That, on the other hand, was something I would never have to worry about. Maybe shot in bed by a woman caught in the act with her husband or boyfriend, but not caught with her. I had no interest in that.

Ever since they mapped the earth standard DNA back in the 21st century, there have been great strides to improve the native DNA of the human race and to selectively turn off the coding for old age and death. Now I know that they can not turn it off completely or conquer death, but they still think that they can add to the original plan to boast our life spans up to about 300 standard earth years. They have been working on that for the last 400 years. That has been since the DNA map of the human genome was completed and the sequence of every base pair was known. Before that, they just tried to stop what was killing us prematurely before old age. Can you imagine, that some 400 years ago the average life span wasn't much more than 70 years. Oh, some people lived to be 100, but most died of old age around 70 and 80. That is just when a young man or woman today is getting into their prime. That was a normal age span, that didn't include the fact that most cancers were not treatable and people still died of disease even when they were in a hospital. I know, sounds like the dark ages and it probably wasn't far removed from that either. Just by a couple of hundred years I figure. But I read somewhere in old books, that 400 years before that, that people died of disease and the life span of the ordinary man was between 20 and 40 years old. Most died of diseases that mankind didn't even understand. They knew nothing of germs and viruses. At first, the few people who were trying to figure it out, were ridiculed and scorned. Worse than the dark ages. They probably ate dirt and walked around naked then too for all I know. Well, everyone being naked could be convenient at times. Probably was good because you had to breed fast before you died or there wasn't going to be any one left alive to carry on the human race, let alone your own family name.

Well, with our family we just naturally had good genes. With the added benefits and advances in gene therapy, we just naturally live a long time unless we get stupid. I finished up in the 10th grade at the ripe old age of 18. Rather than go to additional schooling, I entered the Space Academy which is located in Florida, on the Earth. I spent another five years there and graduated with honors. Not the one located on the moon or proxima centauri. I went to the original old school which has been there for 375 years come next September, 2425. The Space Academy is actually a professional graduate school which gives you the last three years of elective high school subjects designed to give you math and science geared especially for space, physics and other technical courses including computer interfaces, exobiology and hundreds of other things. I can't begin to tell you everything because so much of the memorization was by memory implant. The classes and courses were to teach me how to use the memories and the information that was already implanted in your brain. School was for learning how to use what you already knew. School was not for the purpose of memorizing anything new. They strove for understanding and the ability to apply and use that understanding.

I was fortunate when I first entered school at 5 and I tested as exceptional at a young age. Once I had learned to read and write by age 6 and taken my secondary exams and entered the third grade at 7, the usual age my aptitudes were again reexamined. I tested high in mechanical, scientific and mathematical aptitude. My continued progress from grade 3 through 8, allowed to pursue my education past grade 8. This was the usual grade for all students to graduate and start work unless qualified for further study in high school. I think my grandfather's money could have bought me a few more years of schooling if he wanted it for me, but fortunately I earned it on my own.

Usually by grade 8 at age 16, all pupils get their standard diploma. They are certified to read, write, perform most simple routine mathematics and can work for a living. A woman or a man can legally marry without their parents consent at age 16. After grade 8 they can take special classes in auto mechanics, drafting, electrical or plumbing and similar specialties. I choose to become a space pilot that requires math, science, aeronautics, and a few dozen specialties. I didn't graduate the first time from the Space Academy until I was 20 years old. That included pilot's school which took the better part of a year. I felt like I had gone to school for all my life. I then had to do an internship for at least one year on the run from Earth station (Deep Earth Station), moon, mars, Ganymede[1] run. This was really an exciting thing for a young man who had never been into space. I know that to you old space hands, it is probably a dull and boring routine milk run. I just wanted to get away from home and anywhere off the

---

1   Ganymede is a natural satellite of Jupiter and the largest natural satellite in the Sol solar system. It completes an orbit in a little more than seven days, it is the seventh satellite and third Galilean satellite from Jupiter. Ganymede participates in a 1:2:4 orbital resonance with the satellites Europa and Io respectively. It is larger in diameter than the planet Mercury but has only about half its mass. Ganymede is composed primarily of silicate rock and water ice. It is also fully separated into layers, a differentiated body with an iron-rich, liquid core. At first it was believed that a saltwater ocean exists nearly 200 km below Ganymede's surface, possibly sandwiched between layers of ice. The surface of Ganymede is mostly rock. It used to be pock marked with impact craters some dating back to more than five billion years ago. This forms the habitable portion of Ganymede and is just less than 1/3 of its surface area. The lighter regions of Ganymede comprise the remaining surface area of Ganymede and that is also rock, but has different structural foundations. That portion is also rock, but is not as singular in composition. The scientists believe that later plate tectonic activity resulted in the structural differences of the surface. Ganymede is the only satellite in the Solar System known to possess a magnetosphere. It is believed that this is created by convection currents within a liquid iron core. The small magnetosphere of Ganymede is dwarfed by Jupiter's much larger magnetic field. The satellite originally had a thin oxygen atmosphere that includes oxygen in both it's diatomic and ozone state. Since the taraforming project of 2215, the satellite's levels of oxygen and carbon dioxide have been steadily rising. It can now sustain life a meager thread of life with rich plant life. Ganymede's discovery is credited to Galileo Galilei who observed it in 1610. The satellite's name was given by astronomer Simon Marius in honor of Ganymede the mythological cupbearer of the Greek gods and Zeus's beloved.

planet was fine with me.

You see ever since the 29th amendment to the US Constitution in 2020 giving full citizenship rights to all people regardless of sex and sexual orientation passed, it has been legally acceptable to be homosexual, transgendered person or just about anything. My problem was that my family didn't recognize the US Constitution or at least not the 29th Amendment. Face it, I was the 7th and for there to be an 8th, I had to stick my you know what into a you know what. And to be quite frank with you, I had done it once just on the off chance I was missing something. First, I asked if that was all there was to it. Second, I didn't particularly enjoy it. She was pretty and nice and liked me, but I didn't like her. No, I liked her or I wouldn't have done it with her, but I felt nothing for her. Third, I don't find big tits attractive. With time, they droop, and if you live 150 years, they droop 150 years worth. You get them tightened up every 10 years. By which time you have finally removed enough skin to cover a football field.

The last problem with woman as sex partners, is they all seem to use sex as a tool or weapon to get what they want from you. If they just admitted they liked to screw as much as men did, then the universe would be a much better place. But I am changing this scholarly account of my life into an XXX rated novel. Well, I am going to get to the good stuff, but I thought that even if you no longer have to have any socially redeeming value to the sex stuff, you should at least make a good faith attempt so that posterity will remember you kindly. After all, I am not writing this stuff for the money because one day I will have enough of my own. Right now I have a very generous allowance that could run a small city.

Okay, sex with women is out, because it is boring, dull and doesn't interest me. I like the way guys look, I like the things they have between their legs and most important I like that ever inviting hole they have on the reverse side, just waiting for me to fill it with my presence. I'm sorry. Don't lose interest. I will talk dirty later to keep you interested. In this "lets get acquainted" section, I thought that if someone is reading this 100 years or 200 years from now, when I am dead and gone, I would leave a good impression or at least try to leave a good impression. If you don't like this part, just skip the next 10 pages. I should be getting to the good stuff by then. If you want to completely skip the dull and boring parts, you can skip directly to chapter 3. However, you might have trouble understanding the old slang I use, so try to keep up.

Most people are familiar with the 4 stops I gave earlier of the milk run. We would pilot the big ships of 2 million metric tons or more. They never had to land on the Earth and did not have to escape the Earth's gravity. They were assembled directly in space by Mega Systems, MS for short. The milk run from the Earth was handled usually by elevator car from the Earth up one of the Equatorial Carbon fiber Stalks to the Near Earth Stations around the equator. These had been completed in 2279 and been functioning well for the last 140 years. All the cargo is containerized, and thus the loading and unloading is all done mechanically into the cargo holds of smaller ships. They delivered the cargo to the moon station, Deep Earth Station or cargo ships bound for the outer worlds.

We had the big cargo ship that made the milk run between the near sun destinations. Depending on the orbits, we could make a complete cycle, the order of the stops varying each trip with hyper drive in just under 28 standard days or one lunar not counting loading and unloading time. Yes, I know that you can't really use hyper drive to go faster than the speed of light within a solar system, but we could use it to approach a significant fraction of the speed of light for travel within the solar system. Remember even traveling at half the speed of light is fast. I don't know why I am telling you this as you all learned it in school in the 5th grade. Even if you don't bother to listen or remember it then, why would you remember it now? You can look it up over the ultranet.[2] I usually opt to tie into the local less extensive system where ever I am located. That speed of light thing is such a slow and pesky thing to always have to be waiting on. I wish they would get that fixed. Right now, our hyper drive ships are actually the fastest things in the known universe. So we bring mail and other valuable things to the colonies and worlds outside of the Sol system. We are the equivalent of the Pony Express. Again with the 5th grade history lesson. But if you were like me, you learned it and then promptly forgot it.

I certainly didn't remember what that was, but being in space you pick up certain things that are relevant or at least you hear the old space hands talking about them. The old hands that I ran into on the moon, Earth Station and everywhere like to brag that the Pony

---

2   The current wireless communication between all networked information systems within the Sol solar system including out to the outer orbits of Pluto and the like. Good for up to one light year of Sol, but who has that long to wait.

Express was the only connection with civilization that many of the old west towns had; and they, as space faring men, brought the only contact with civilization that people on the outer reaches of the settled systems within 5 to 10 parsecs[3] of Earth have to date. At the time of this writing we have not settled anything further than 15 parsecs from Earth. I know that we are pushing that back each decade, but the limitations right now are on finding good Earth type planets. Planets that are capable of supporting life as we know it, which are orbiting a sun that will not roast you alive or freeze your nuts off, and has a magnetosphere that will protect you from the solar winds, radiation and all the common hazards of space. Forget about the gamma ray bursts and the black holes that nothing can protect you from. It's the old saying, you pays your money and you takes your chances.

The more places that man can plant his seed and it takes root; the more likely we are to survive any calamity on a planet wide basis. To lose the Earth as a habitat would be horrendous and might put mankind back a thousand years, but we would still exist and survive. It is our greatest resource of technology and raw materials. But as little as 300 years ago, It would have been the end of mankind. Not a pretty picture. Today we could repopulate the Earth from the outer colonies if some gamma ray burst killed all animal life and mankind on Earth and in the Sol system. It would be difficult and take many generations, but it could be done. 300 years ago there would not have been enough biodiversity from the moon and space stations to accomplish the feat, assuming the people on them had not been wiped out with the people on the Earth. Plus the people on the moon and other off world colonies, were not sufficient in numbers nor could they sustain themselves. They required the resources of the earth to subsidize them.

I don't know about you, but right about now my head is hurting trying to remember all these facts. I leave the rest to the professors. I will fill you in on certain things if I feel some explanation is necessary.

---

3   A parsec is a unit of distance measurement equal to about 3.26 light years. The **parsec** ("parallax of one arcsecond" symbol pc) is a unit of length, equal to just over 30 trillion kilometers, or about 3.26 light years. The parsec is used in astronomy. The parsec is defined as the length of the adjacent side of an imaginary right triangle in space. The two dimensions that this triangle is based on are the angle (which is defined as 1 arcsecond, and the opposite side (which is defined as 1 Astronomical Unit which is the distance from the Earth to the sun). Using these two measurements, along with the rules of trigonometry, the length of the adjacent side (the parsec) can be found. The first use of the term "parsec" was in an astronomical publication in 1913, and attributed to Herbert hall Turner.

I remember that this is a hard core rated story and many of you people who appreciate hard core shit, either didn't learn this stuff or promptly forgot it after they told you about it. I would have except I always knew I wanted to go into space and not just hump my wife or some woman in my spare time for the next 130 years between eating, sleeping and going to work. I don't have to learn anything, but I want to be constantly doing something new and different and going interesting places. And I have to admit that for the first couple of trips, Deep Earth Station, the moon, mars, and Ganymede are interesting and can be lots of fun. But I am getting ahead of my story. I am still 20 and I have one year of internship on the milk run. This is the beginning of my story or part of it.

They had wiped out all known social diseases and had mandatory vaccinations before you entered school, and again at puberty. Mankind had eliminated most pesky diseases or kept them under control. There were complete physicals and genetic mapping of all off world visitors with quarantine. Going out into space meant that you basically had a sexual license to do what you wanted to do with whoever wanted to do it with you. If you got your jollies only with 4 people doing you at the same time, one of them being male, one of them being female and two of them being over the age of consent, which is off world 16 as it is on earth, then you were free to contract with those people. Or you could get them for free if you could persuade them to do it with you. Then, have a great time. You paid your room tax, other taxes for the liquor, and all the other adult pleasures, so enjoy them. While there is still some smoking on Earth, it is strictly banned in space. You can't buy it, sell it, make it, grow it or do anything with anything that burns in space. Just too damn dangerous. Plus, it plays havoc with the air filtration systems. You need an entire planet's ecosystem to filter out all that crap in the air and we just don't have it on our ships or stations. They also banned it from the colonies because the health costs were too expensive.

Sure we cured cancer and we can now clone lungs and kidneys and other organs, but the cost is steep, plus you lose several months of working time getting over the operations. Society just put its foot down and said enough is enough. It is illegal on Earth, but for enough money you can usually get what you want. Same with some of the illegal drugs. But that stuff is its own punishment. You burn yourself out and the doctors can test for it and that automatically disqualifies you for corrective medical care. Oh sure, you can get help to get off the drugs and once you are clean for a year, you can get an operation, but by the time that you know you need to get off, it is too late. Most addicts burn out and die within three years of getting on the stuff. That is because the stuff you can get now is so powerful, that you live about 150 years worth in 3 years. I sometimes think the government puts out the powerful stuff just to get rid of the people who won't learn. Thank you, I will take my life in small dosages over all those 150 years, and not cram it all into 3 years.

They tell me that the shit they take makes them forget all about sex. The people who are addicted are not the least bit interested in sex. Man, what a pathetic way to go. Me, I seem to do my best thinking with my sex organ. I am getting ahead of my story, but I always did enter the room about 20 centimeters (that's about 8 inches for you who still think on the old American system-just under 8) ahead of myself. I am proud of my endowment because we are not genetically enhanced, that is the size of my male member and the size of my father to hear him tell it and the size of his father. Sure, for a few hundred thousand, we could have been given 23 or 26 cm, but my eyes are the biggest sex organ I have. When I look at a dick I want to look at all the big ones, but you are not coming near me with anything over 20 cm to put it anywhere in me. I don't usually like anything in me anyway, but for the right person anything is possible. Fortunately for me, I have never met that fictitious right person yet. And while I talk a lot, my mouth isn't that big either.

Chapter Two

This is not autobiographical. That was a word a friend of mine told me to use. He said it is a technical term that means the story of my life. He finished in English and Technical Writing whereas I finished in Science and Math and learned to pilot. I am not supposed to be writing this book because to write books you have to finish in English and have some writing specialty and skills. I don't care, and if I can't get published because of that, then I guess I am really a writer at heart. I write because I have to write. I need to sit down and write something because my head is full of ideas and most importantly, it turns me on. Not the stuff I am supposed to write, but the stuff I actually write about. Or the stuff I will write when we get to the good parts. Wait, I am getting there now.

I don't want to go all the way back to my childhood, because I am sure all parents have pictures of junior grabbing his weenie and playing with it. I simply don't remember much before I hit puberty; but when I hit it, I really hit it and hit it hard. Once my penis, that's another technical term, started to grow, it grew and I lost interest in just about everything except servicing my penis. Look, since the beginning of time, boys have names for their penis. I would continue to use the common names, but for some reason the older names seem dirtier to me. I don't like to flaunt my special knowledge or information, but I got that from dating a male nurse. We never had sex, but we fooled around a little. That was later in my life at the Academy and we haven't gotten to that yet. He loved to shock and amuse me with the technical terms and the old earth slang for the same term. Mostly it confused me.

I have read books from the past in the library and learned that a penis used to be called a Dick, Richard, Johnson, fuck tool, man tool, third leg, baby maker, and all sorts of names. I prefer to use them because the terms we use today seem sterile and clean. I want this book to read as dirty and enjoyable as possible. Therefore, I will use whatever terms set me off at the moment. In case you can't figure it out, I will make the term obvious when I use it. If there is any doubt, I will spell it out. I know you can read, because this book does not have any pictures. Not that anyone can't get pictures of sex, of anyone with anyone else. Man with women, man with man, woman with woman, and any multiple of that in any ratio of people. The problem is that it is just sex and pictures of sex. Once the shrinks get hold of a sex novel, they make everything so consensual and take all the fun out of it. Believe me all the sex was consensual, but I know I pushed the limits of credibility. The sole purpose of this is so that you can place yourself in my position and almost feel that you actually did these things. I don't have any trouble putting myself in these positions because I did actually do these things.

I first knew that I was not like my friends in school during the mandatory physical training classes. This wasn't until about the 7th grade when I was about 12. You see that was when I started to develop as a man. I had lots of friends, but I had one friend in particular. We fooled around a little. Well, actually a lot. We kept this up as we both tested to continue our education while our friends slowly dropped out or took specialty classes for different trades. We laughed at them. Some were married before or by the age of 18 and working jobs. The rest were married by the time we graduated at age 20. Why not, a steady piece of ass, that's old time slang for fucking (having sex) with a girl. I love these old time terms because they are so powerful when you hear them or read them. Having sex sounds like something you do in a hospital or a classroom. Fucking sounds dirty, that's why I like the old term. I think it originated when America was just a young country. The word is banned in normal print and has not come down to us to mean down and dirty sex.

Anyway, I have given you enough of this history lesson for now. I learned this stuff because reading about sex is fun, especially when you can't do it or have done it and you are waiting up until you can do it again. I still haven't figured out why they call it a piece of ass, unless the man was putting his dick up the woman's ass hole (that's the old term for anus or elimination hole.) See I tell you these old terms are so much better at getting you ready for sex than what we have been taught as the terms to use. Anyway, I had never heard of anyone putting his dick up someone's ass hole before and never gave it thought. At the time my friend, whom I will call Tobert, because I don't kiss and tell or fuck and tell, he and I were discovering sex. Sex with each other. Well, Tobert and I used to fool around and talk about the women we wanted to have sex with, and maybe have a child with if we were approved and her fertility initiated at a clinic. For the longest time we just fooled around with each other using our hands and one day, just out of the blue we thought about and then talked putting our mouths on each other instead of our hands, and we discovered oral sex. We started blowing each other. That's another old term. It sounds dirty just to hear it when compared to the term oral sex. Again, I don't know why they call it a blow job, because the person giving oral sex doesn't blow. Now know that it helps more if they suck. We were content to blow each other for the longest time. Then I kept growing and Tobert couldn't get all of me into his mouth. Yet I wanted him to swallow all of me. It just wasn't going to happen.

The more I thought about it the more I wanted to be able to put all of my dick into Tobert's mouth, but it just wasn't going to fit. I thought that probably that was why men fucked women, their hole was bigger and deeper, definitely deeper than a mouth. So one day as I was thinking about fucking a woman. I wanted to find one that perhaps looked like a man or like Tobert. I thought about fucking Tobert but did not know how to accomplish that. I kind of figured that there must be a way because in sex class they taught us that some people like to have sex with other people of the same sex. They had that right under the Constitution, but they never told us how they accomplished the dirty deed. We knew all about women's vaginas and men's penises, but how two men or two women have sex, they conveniently left out much to our inconvenience. But I knew that there had to be a way. Then It dawned on me. I wanted to fuck Tobert up his ass hole. I wanted to put my penis, I mean my dick, up his ass hole and move it back and forth until I had my orgasm. I wanted to shoot my male seed up inside of a real live person and not into my hand, Tobert's hand or even his mouth.

Well, the rest is all history. I won't bore you with the details because the first few times were rather messy. First, we couldn't figure how to get my big thing up his tiny hole. We pushed, or I pushed and he held firm and we tried for twenty minutes. It hurt me and nothing slid in. I remembered that women make a natural lubrication. I found something that would make things slippery. Finally I got in and Tobert was crying because he said it hurt. I told him to take it like a man and that I would let him do me when I finished with his ass. Of course I made sure I used my hands and took care of Tobert so that when I shot my seed off inside of him he shot his seed from my manual manipulation of him. Then he didn't want to do me. He was satisfied. We did that the next time also. And time and time again, I would fuck him and made sure he climaxed. We had to be careful because we almost got caught several times. Each time I would do Tobert first and make sure he had his orgasm when I had mine, and then he never wanted to fuck me. He couldn't and that went on for years. I was happy and so was Tobert, I think.

When we both graduated I was fucking Tobert almost every day and loving it. Tobert was loving every inch of me. He loved for me to put my dick up his ass hole and fuck him until I came. He usually came at the same time. We had started kissing and eventually learned to face each other while we were fucking. You see, at first, the purpose was for me to get my dick up his ass hole and the best route to his ass hole was from his back side. When we graduated to fucking for mutual pleasure, we figured out how to fuck while facing each other. Then we added kissing, touching, biting necks and ears and all sorts of what is called foreplay. I don't know why the old term is foreplay because it only involved two people not four. But we got to be very good at this. We didn't need to get married because we were fucking as much as any married couple. Couple of faggots that is. A faggot is one half of an M-M couple. A fagot is a man who likes another man for a sexual partner, just as a M-M likes men and an M-W is called a straight person, regardless of their sex.

We were very happy all through school because we were both getting as much sex as we wanted even if we couldn't sleep together. By that age, having a friend sleep over of the same sex was out of the question. I could have invited some of my friends that were girls, but boys, was still a taboo subject. That is the old term for something "against the social order" or just "ATSO." We used to call them "at so's" rules. Obviously they encouraged you to fuck your brains out with the right people. You can have your constitutional guaranteed rights, but don't push them. I read in a book somewhere that all people were created equal, but it seemed that some people were more equal than others. I never could figure that one out.

It broke my heart when Tobert left for his career. He had studied space law and would be working at first trying to get criminals off and later work his way up to some good lawyer job where he didn't have to deal with criminals. Well, I say that it broke my heart, but actually what it broke was my spirit. I was used to fucking every day and now all I could do was to beat my head against the wall. I knew I needed to get off the Earth to get away from my family. That way if I engaged in any extracurricular activities, word would not get back to them. It was permissible to be a man and a man couple anywhere, but it was not as socially accepted like a man and a woman couple. You were supposed to register your preference if you wanted the protection of the law. Well, I registered as still a virgin and went to the counseling classes from the time I was 12 until I graduated and swore that I was a virgin. I did confess that I masturbated a lot. The government would have paid for me to have a professional woman to service me once a month under the health plan, but I declined saying I was saving myself for marriage. That was not one of those perjury things. I was glad because if they had ever used one of those reliability meters on me, I probably, no I know, that every bell and whistle would have gone off.

So I took the milk run off Earth for my internship and started my career and my hunt for a good piece of ass. See, when I use the term, I really mean a piece of ass. Why is it so difficult for the old terms to mean what they say? Today you offer a man a piece of ass, he knows that maybe you want to sell him an animal that is a cross between two other animals, a cut of meat or whatever. He will not have the slightest idea that you are talking about having sex. You know, fucking. He certainly will not think that you want to put your dick up his ass hole or vice versa. He wouldn't consider it and of course wouldn't let you do it to him in a million years. And I didn't have a million years to wait. Not only was I impatient, I was fucking horny. That means I wanted to fuck any ass hole that would let me at this point. I thought about getting a girl, but quickly lost my erection. My dick wouldn't cooperate. So much for my brief chapter about my early sexual conquests, I really didn't not have any. I didn't have but one, and I even worried what Tobert was going to do. He probably would register as a man seeking a man and try to find someone with a penis big enough to satisfy him and settle down and be happy.

As for me, I wasn't going to admit anything; I was just looking for my next piece of ass. I was also trying to keep from getting caught by my family. I was going off the Earth to find a steady piece of ass. What I didn't realize is that there is a great big world and an even bigger off world out there. Sex is everywhere and you can do it with anyone that wants you and being married is just a convenience for the people. However, I am getting ahead of my story. My next stop, up the Equatorial Carbon Fiber Stalks to Near Earth Station (NES.) I read that in an old book, some writer had predicted these Carbon fiber Stalks and they called them beanstalks in the slang. Came from some old nursery rhyme or story about some guy who had magic beans and they grew into a giant beanstalk that went up into the sky. The boy climbed the beanstalk to another land up in the clouds and met a giant. How silly can you get. All the old space dogs call them the beanstalks.

The trip up the beanstalk is boring. The cargo goes up one side and the empty container goes down the other. The cargo is containerized, that means it fits into a certain container size. The containers are actually quite big about 7 meters by about 10 meters. That is a little cramped for people, but the secret there is the transportation authority has compartments that are like double-decker containers. They are still about 7x10 meters, but instead of being 10 meters high, they are actually about 30 meters high. The standard 10 meters high, the height of the second container, and the distance between containers of about 10 meters. This means it is like living in a townhouse which is about 6 stories high with sleeping and rest room facilities and lounging areas for the passengers. This keeps the fares to Near Earth Station, NES, reasonable.

The trip takes a total of about 15 hours and then you have the waiting and screening process. Remember, there are still some people who are not happy with the new world government. Every country has their own sovereignty, but when everyone has enough food to eat, a job and a house or something to live in that is comfortable, you still have people who are not happy. We don't have much in the way of people using explosives or something like that, but with 2.5 billion people on the Earth, that being the number that the government figured was the limit that the planet could reasonably support and not over tax the system, you are bound to get someone who is unhappy. You just can't please all the people all the time. That is a catchy saying, and perhaps

I ought to get some credit for thinking it up.

A Boner Book

Chapter Three

Well, the trip up the beanstalk was fun. However, at first I thought I was absolutely going out of my mind. The trip up or down takes about 15 hours as I said. What occupied my free time during the waiting to be processed was a young man I saw. This young man was apparently traveling with his parents. He was not too old, about 18, and he should have been working or married, but he was with his parents. He was above the age of consent and he looked mighty tasty. I didn't think we would ever hook up, but my divining rod, that's another old term for a stick or branch of a tree that was used to find water. My divining rod didn't find water, but had sniffed out a hole. My divining rod, my dick, had found a hole for me that it wanted to pump and perhaps see if it could find water or something in that hole. It wanted the chance to drill the hole. And if I had any input, I would cooperate fully. We waited in the staging area together. We had already been screened, and they usually send passengers in groups. Each townhouse could comfortably accommodate about 24 single people or even 24 couples in an emergency situation. The lower 4 floors of the compartments were individualized sleeping rooms. The two upper floors were lounge areas with mechanized food dispensers. You could eat, sit and talk to people and your fellow passengers and even watch television. The lower four floors of the compartments were individualized sleeping rooms. They were very comfortable for one person but also designed big enough for two people to share such as a husband and a wife. They would be a little cramped, but the sleeping platform was big enough for two people. However, it was not big enough for three and any child would be assigned his own compartment. At least anyone over the age of, I think about 8, gets their own compartment.

I would get my own and so would cutie. Assuming we were in the same townhouse. While you have assigned times, those times are approximate as they like to keep the weight going up on the beanstalk computed to equal what comes down and not to overload the going out traffic they wanted the inbound and out bound traffic to balance each other. That is not usually a problem, because the computers know your weight and when they place you as available they assign you a number and you go when that number is posted on the board. They did not seem to have very many people assigned to this time slot. This was not a high tourist time or season. There was always travel up the beanstalks, but there were three of them around the globe and only so many people going up. Remember what goes up usually has to come down. I am filled with these catchy phrases. I should be writing these down. I guess I am now. I hadn't thought about it.

I thought that all the people here right now were probably going in the same bucket. They call the units on the beanstalk a bucket, because like a bucket, it is filled with stuff to bring somewhere. I know that at first, everything that went off world had to be scrutinized to 10 to the 10th power. When we started colonizing the moon, we made our own dirt in the underground caverns off world and then added back soil cultures to make the sterile dirt able to grow plants and crops. We didn't want any of the bad bacteria in the soil from Earth to infect the moon and all the other planets. And we still don't. Mankind has traveled quite some distance, but we have found no life on any other planet. No other life than ours in the explored universe. Granted we know less than 1/1,000,000 of 1 percent or even less of the galaxy, but all life we have found has all originated on Earth and been brought by man around to where man has gone. We bring our shit with us and I guess it is good. All waste, especially human waste is highly valued. It is collected, digested, sterilized and then used to make the dirt we produce on the moon and other planets more fertile. Nothing like some real organic material to beef up all that dead, crushed rock. A messy job, but somebody has to do it and it pays a fair wage. On Earth the reprocessing is all done by machines with people running them. I am sure that the systems I studied, just to know about them in my work, required a lot of manual input on small installations off world. But here on earth, mother nature does most of the messy work and we only have to supervise the process.

There was a funny joke I read about in an old book when

people still believed in God creating life on Earth. Well, maybe there is a God, and maybe he did create life because we still have not scientifically found out where life came from. Oh sure, we know in theory, but we still can't create life from scratch and probably never will. The old story goes that a scientist was talking to God himself. The man said that man was as powerful as God because man could create life, just like God did. Supposedly in the Bible, that's the book that many of the churches still believe in, that God took some clay and fashioned Adam. He was the first man and God made him out of clay and breathed life into him. The scientist said that he could take clay and subject it to certain atmospheres, some electricity through lightning or something and produce the building blocks of life. From those original building blocks, make amino acids and create life and eventually one-celled organisms. The scientist then said that through evolution, he could create more complicated forms of life and multiple cell animals and then animals and eventually create a man from the clay like God did. God looked at the scientist and said, "Get your own clay!" So much for the old humor.

Well, I was right, we were all put in the same bucket and everyone sat in the lounge area as required during attachment and for the first ten minutes until we reached the pressurized ceiling. They of course have to pressurize the buckets that carry passengers or within ten minutes we would all be dead. The cargo buckets are not pressurized unless the cargo demands it. This would be some food stuffs and certain machinery. Those items may have to be pressurized, but they are usually in a nitrogen atmosphere that will not support combustion and even then they are sometimes shipped at one half or one quarter atmosphere. Depending on the cargo, the cargo containers may be pressurized. People are shipped at about .8 atmospheres. Nothing more than the equivalent of an altitude of about 3,000 meters. That is why we have to stay in the lounge to make sure the pressurized cabin holds up. The two buckets that make up the townhouse have three airlocks that close automatically in the event that we lose pressurization, and there are oxygen thanks everywhere for us, on each level. You don't want to have time to run around looking for oxygen when you have a pressure leak.

I read one time about a massive system failure on the stalk transport many years ago, and when they opened the bucket they had 45 dead citizens. There was hell to pay for that error. Because of that accident, in the last 100 years, they have not lost anyone from a pressure leak or system failure. Some people die on the way out from heart attacks, strokes, aneurysms and medical conditions that they knew before they got in the buckets. They were traveling off world so they could enjoy a lower gravity. We can artificially create a gravity of double what you have or about ½ Earth normal, but we can't block gravity. That would take machines too big to put off world. One day we will be able to do it, but not just yet. We are working on it. Little by little we are unraveling the secrets of the Universe as we find more and more of the universe in our back yard.

I had observed cutie, whose name I found out later was Jonathan, and he went by the name John. He said people had less trouble with a simple name. I had even less trouble with cute guys with simple names who simply knew what they wanted. I had followed him to the rest room while we were at the station, and I observed him pull out a nice piece of meat, not that I was interested in that side of him, but it is fun to play with while you take care of business with the other side. He looked at me and saw that I had looked at him. He even let me see what he had, and I of course made sure that he could see what I had. I was trying to get my fish to swallow my hook. From the way his eyes popped out, I think he liked my hook. We sanitized our hands in the "sani." unit, and walked out. I was still adjusting myself as his attention caused me to start to unfold my hook to its full potential. Translated to old speak, my dick was getting hard, hard as a rock and looking for somewhere to go and hide. Preferably some nice warm, wet ass hole to hide in and deposit his love offering. I wanted to pump that little boy full of my cum until it came out his throat. I smiled and didn't say a word.

I kept looking at him every few minutes while in the lounge portion of the bucket to let him know that I was still interested. We sat there strapped in for the first ten minutes until we were release to go about our affairs. I immediately looked at John and went to the lowest level and punched in my sleeping code and opened the door to my little private sleeping room that was just big enough for a sleeping platform, a place to relieve myself and some drinking water and a mirror. I held back to see if John was following me. He had wandered down trying to appear as if he was looking for a sleeping room. I looked over at him and asked him if he had a room. He shook his head no, and asked if he wanted to share one. There was no one else around. He said yes and walked in. The fly walked willingly into the web of the spider. I was one happy spider.

I turned and locked the door. I looked at him and we exchanged names and he said he had never done anything like this before. I told him I had not either, I know I am a liar, but so what. If you had seen him and his pretty face, you would have sold your own mother to get to him. He had a pretty face, was just short of 2 meters tall and his body told me he was either a naturally athletic type or he actually was an athlete, and perhaps competed in sports such as swimming or gymnastics. His body was fucking beautiful and not to be believed in its smoothness. I guess that is the same thing. Whatever, I was pleased with my catch. I would be reliving this over and over again in my dreams. I set up my holographic camera on the dresser and tried to inconspicuously turn it on. It would record for the next 24 hours if I didn't turn it off again. It is a shame, that the reasonably priced cameras can only record up to 24 hours on a memcard. I am watching the play back of that encounter as I write this. Perhaps that is why I will be giving such an exacting description of the events.

As we enter the room, I turn on the lights so that when I set the camera it will have enough light to file everything. It has the darkness attachment, but even then it still requires some light, even if only a minimum amount. John's hair is what I guess people would call dirty blond. It is not light enough to be blond, but it is a light golden brown and is mostly straight. His eyes are a funny color. One is light blue and the other is sort of a hazel color. His eyes were not brown in color, but a much lighter color. His skin is lightly tanned, but not very much. Just enough not to be pasty white. He is wearing a pullover shirt, standard space issue as are all of our clothes. We left all our earth clothing at home as everything in space is made to be cleaned in space or consumed and disposed of in our disposal systems. Same for our pants and underclothing. Our boots are space regulation issue with anti skid soles that leave no skid marks and have magnetic inserts in the soles to enable us to grip any metallic surface. Sure we have some sort of artificial gravity but you never know when you need the ability to grip the surface you are walking on, especially when the wall becomes the floor.

First, I gather him in my arms and then lean my head toward his and we kiss. His lips are soft and moist and tell me he is ready for me. I hold him and his soft lips allow my tongue entrance into his warm moist mouth. I feel his teeth and the softness of his tongue as it meets mine. I am not sure I know what the term love means, but if you were to ask me at this moment in time, I would have to tell you I love this boy. I have been without human companionship and the touch of another human being for almost four months now.

When I lift his shirt off him, I see the smoothest, pretty skin I have ever seen and two beautiful male nipples staring me in the face. Obviously my initial assessment of him is accurate. He has the body of a swimmer and possibly also has an interest in gymnastics. His chest appears to be one big slab of muscle over a beautifully classical young man's body. His teeth are perfect and he seems naturally at home and at ease with his shirt off. I unfasten his belt and lower his pants for him. At the same time I remove his underwear. They are regulation white issue for off world. Dyes mess up the reprocessing systems and they complicate the cleaning process. Forget all that hype about new scientific age colors and cleaning solutions on Earth. That is all just advertising hype. He steps out of his pants and removes his boots himself. I start to unbutton my shirt and he says, "Here, let me do that. This is the first time I have ever undressed anyone before. I have always wanted to undress a man. A man all my own for me to play with and do whatever I want with him." I look into his eyes and I melt. He is so sweet and likable.

"I am here for you to play with. We have about 14 hours free if your parents won't be looking for you." I wanted him for more than 14 hours, but would settle for that. I must confess that pilot's training has kept me in good shape and I have always had a natural build that ran in my family. I bent a little to make it easier to remove my shirt and then his hands moved to my belt. It too was regulation, and he had no trouble removing it. He quickly lowered my pants and underwear at the same time. I removed my boots and socks. When we were naked as the day we were born, I held him and we kissed again. My tongue again probed the inner recesses of his mouth. We were both hard as a rock and at that instant very much in love. "Come over here and let us lay down together." I told him. He followed my suggestion and then we lay down on the sleeping platform.

"Take my head in your hands again and kiss me some more." He asked in almost a pleating fashion.

"Have you ever been with another guy before?" I wondered.

"Never. I wanted to many times, but I didn't want to declare myself since I am an only child and it would hurt my parents not to have a grandchild." He whispered.

"You could still have a child." I said.

"No. It would not be the same. They want me to marry and have a large family and visit at holidays and play with grandchildren. And I just don't see that happening. Especially now." He said as he looked up at me.

"Why do you say that?" I wanted to know.

"Because now that I am holding a real live true man in my arms, I know that this is the right thing for me."

"This is your first time. How can you say that?" I was being put on the spot.

"Because when I held naked girls in my arms, it didn't feel anything as good as this. It didn't feel good. Nothing ever felt this good before." He stopped and looked at me. "I now know what I have been wanting is a naked man in my arms to be with, to play with, and to make love to. This is what I have wanted since I first realized there was such a thing as sex. I can't explain it. I just feel it and know it." It was obvious he knew that he liked men. Now just how far would he go to please one. I wanted him to be happy, but I wanted to fuck his pretty little ass hole and teach him how to please the only real plaything of a man.

I have to tell you now that there was a barbaric custom in some parts of the world and in some religions where they used to cut off part of the male penis at birth. You hear me right. I am not making this up. They cut off part of the skin around the penis as part of a religious ceremony. How barbaric. There were even some tribes in I think it was Africa and thereabouts, where they used to cut off the female sex organ to keep a woman faithful. How horrible. The world government put a stop to those practices thank you. Now if a man has trouble with the skin tightening around the head of his dick, he can get it surgically cut back to make the opening bigger, but they do not remove it. The literature said that women for years wanted the men to be what was called circumcised for hygiene purposes.

BULLSHIT. That's old slang for cow droppings. It was meant to signify the utter worthlessness of a remark. Actually, cow droppings are valuable for their organic compounds today, and especially off world. They taught little boys to wash behind their ears and to brush their teeth. They could certainly teach them to wash the skin around their dick and to keep it clean. How would they like it if all the men decided to mutilate all the little girls in the name of hygiene? Women would be up in arms against men. Yet for centuries, no, actually thousands of years, the women decided to have the end of the penis' skin cut off. The justification, because they thought that there was too much skin and it was easier to keep clean this way.

Well, neither John nor I have had any skin cut off the end of our dicks. So I held him in my arms and kissed him all over his body, and enjoyed taking in my view his entire naked body, just as the day he was born, only grown up. I lifted his arms and he had a nice tuff of hair under each arm. I smell and inhaled his fragrance. Sure I smelled his antiodorant, but I also smelled him. It was there, under the fragrance. His clean young boy smell that excited me. The hair under his arms was long and rather straight. I kissed it and he moved.

"That tickles." He said in defense of his movement.

"Yes, but it does feel good, doesn't it."

"Unbelievably so." Then I licked him there. His eyes rolled, his head turned toward me, and he found my mouth. Then he kissed me deep and hard.

"You like the taste of yourself?"

"When it is on your lips. I don't know why, but you taste wonderful."

"That's you, you're tasting." I smiled and licked the inside of his mouth. I then bend down and took his dick in my mouth and ran my tongue around under the skin around the head of his dick. He was a nice size, about 17 cm in length and big around. He tasted of young boy, my favorite flavor. He was leaking fluid like a running tap. I didn't want him to climax too soon so I stood up and he raised my arms and began to lick and chew under my arms. First one, then the other.

"You're right. You taste delicious. I want to eat you alive. Or at least take little nibbles." He smiled as he said that. Then he bent down and took my dick into his mouth. He did as I had done to him. He ran his tongue around under my foreskin and tickled the head of my dick. It was wonderful and I thought that I might shoot just from this. I stopped him. Then I kissed him again.

"I want to place my love deep inside of you." He looked puzzled.

"What do you mean?" Apparently he didn't understand that

two guys could fuck. I didn't know how to explain it to him.

"I want to place my love inside of you." Again he looked puzzled. "Spread your legs for me." I instructed him. I put my arms between his legs and moved my head between his legs and spread the cheeks of his butt. I went straight for his tiny pink puckered opening and ran my tongue across his ass hole.

"Oh, I didn't know anything could feel that grand." I knew he was hooked, if I didn't frighten him away. I resumed eating out his ass hole and he spread my legs and returned the favor for me at the same time. "You smell and taste funny there. The smell seems to be you. Just like the smell under your arms. You, but more so you and it makes me even harder." This kid was turning out to be a real butt sniffer, dick licker and man worshiper. I knew I liked him. "You taste so good. I want to stick my tongue all the way inside of you." Oh, I knew that would feel good.

"Go ahead. Enjoy yourself." I gave him free rein to tongue fuck me all he wanted.

"You don't mind?"

"How does it feel when I do it to you?"

"If feels strange and great. I don't know why. I never thought two guys could lick each other there and give each other pleasure. I only thought about rubbing a penis to give me pleasure. I have always wanted to touch and rub my friends, but I knew they would probably not approve. I had not registered as a man-man (M-M) and so did not wear any symbol identifying me as such. I had seen lots of people wearing the symbol to make it easier to identify sex partners, but I didn't want to do that yet. It would crush my parents." I had him hooked. He wanted me and I wanted him.

"There are more things that two guys can do together. I will show you later, but right now I want to suck on your dick some more. I want you to do the same to me, if you want. And when you cum I want to drink down your discharge."

"You can do that and it won't make you sick?" Ah, he was curious.

"Of course you can, and it will taste delicious." I will drink you down and if you want you can drink me down. Trust me. You will love it." We started our oral assault on each other's dicks. I ran my tongue around the head again, and then put my lips around the base of the head under his skin. Then I pulled the skin gently down the shaft of his dick and began the up and down motions that are so familiar to boys everywhere. We had not been at it more than about a minute when I could feel him getting close and I stepped up the pace and then he filled my mouth full of the sweetest tasting boy cream I had ever tasted. He had never cum with anyone before according to him, and I would believe it. He came so quickly and so much, that I believed he was telling me the truth. The taste of him filled my mouth, and was all the mental stimulation I needed to shoot my seeds into his mouth. He gagged a little because of the volume, but he swallowed it all and looked up at me with a shit eating grin.

"You are right again. This tastes just like you too, only more so than your arms or elimination hole."

"Did you know that in the old stories, that used to be called your ass hole. It sounds dirtier to me when you say it that way. The sound is more forbidden and therefore more fun."

"No, I didn't know that. I like the sound of that, and I think you are right. What we are doing is not forbidden nor do I think it is bad. But when you think about how good and how right it feels, it seems so much more secretive and forbidden to think about it as being dirty and nasty to do. I like feeling that way with you. It makes doing it even more fun."

"Here" I motioned to him to come to my arms. He swung around and I held him in my embrace. "I want to hold you and kiss you."

"Now, while my mouth still has some of you inside of it."

"Especially now. Kiss me and show me how much you liked what we just did." I kissed him and ran my tongue around inside of his mouth. I know he could taste his own baby seeds in my mouth. They just don't all get swallowed, no matter how hard you try. I looked into his eyes and instantly fell for this little boy. I say little boy, he was a man and could legally have married two years ago without his parents consent. I held him in my arms and we kissed and hugged. I had adjusted the temperature so that there was no need to pull a cover over us. I didn't want the cover to block the holocorder. I wanted to know all the things this kid did to me while I was asleep. I would just have to be careful to encode the access strip to this recording. I would cherish the memory of this meeting for a long time. "We can continue after we get a little rest. Close your eyes and rest with me, and then we can start again later when we are again fresh and ready for more love. And while I sleep, if you want to touch me, feel me, and hold me;

then just do so." He looked at me questioning me. Again I told him. "Feel free to do so. Not only do I want to please you, it would make me feel good too. Right now I am here to please you, and while you are asleep I may hold and touch you also. Is that all right."

"Yes. I want you to do that. I don't want to have to tell you or even ask you. Just do it. I don't know if I can sleep with you next to me. I am so excited about having you here. I want to touch and feel you all over."

"Then do so. My body is yours right now. Touch me, feel me, lick me, suck me and play with me all you want. I want to be the stuff of your dreams in your future. I have more things planned for us, and I think we need a little rest before we start. What ever you do, do not have another climax without me. If you have to, wake me up first." I held him in my arms and placed my head on my pillow. I closed my eyes and promptly fell into a light sleep. I always want to sleep after I have had a climax. I fell asleep with him rubbing and feeling all parts of my body, running his hands over my skin, fondling my dick, and playing with my tits. I knew I was his living "man doll" to play with for this time.

Despite the fact that he couldn't keep his hands off me, I drifted off into a light sleep and rested. The change in pressure and the sex had actually worn me out. I think that John was tired too. I awoke about an hour or more later to hear John breathing in my face, and his arms and hands holding me close to him. He also had a slightly hard dick so I know that he was somewhat aroused. His free hand was grabbing my dick, and balls and that was the position in which he had fallen asleep. I didn't want to disturb his peaceful slumber. Even now, much later, I did not edit out any of the recorded things that happened while we slept. Those moments were too precious for him for me to just discard them.

He awoke a little later to see me staring into his eyes. He looked up and kissed me, and then started rubbing my dick. I asked him, "Are you horny now?" An obvious question since the answer was poking me in my stomach.

"What does that mean?" He looked puzzled.

"Another old time slang term. I like to use them because they are so guttural and dirty sounding. Also nobody else seems to know them. It is like it is my secret language. It means that your dick is hard and you want sex." He shook his head yes.

"Teach me your secret language. I want to learn everything." An eager pupil and a more than willing dirty old man as a teacher I thought. Sorry reader, more old slang.[4]

"There is something more exciting to do right now that I want to teach you."

"Please teach me. Just tell me what to do and I will do it." He was so tempting and so beautiful and so eager to please. I just wanted to eat him up and devour him forever. I had to be careful. I could care about this boy. The first chance I get to meet people and I fall for the first one I meet. Something is wrong with me or I keep getting lucky meeting good people.

"I am afraid. It will cause you some pain at first, and then feel so good after a while. Actually, it will begin to feel real good, and you won't understand it." He looked confused.

"What do you mean, cause me some pain, and then I will feel good."

"Well, I want to place my love inside of you."

"You said that before, what do you mean."

"I want to fuck you. That means I want to have sex with you just as if you were a woman."

"But you can't, I'm not a girl." This is most people's first reaction. Or at least people who are not sexually experienced in man-man sex.

"I can. You will like it, and it will feel good to you. I can show you."

"Will you be gentle with me and not hurt me." He wanted so much to please me. I didn't want to hurt him, but I wanted to show him this pleasure. I was hard again and ready to fuck him. I reached into my travel kit and took out the lubricant. "This stuff will make it possible, and keep any pain to a minimum."

"What's that?" He wanted to know everything.

"It is the same stuff that men and women use to make sure that

---

4   The term meant an older person who took advantage of younger and sometimes underage people for sex. Today people look young with nice skin and such well until they get to be over a hundred. The hormone shots and periodic Maser surgery can tighten up anything that sags and remove skin where the scar barely shows. I knew old was really meaning more experienced, but really old was someone who was close to death. We looked and performed at our prime until a few years before we die. Science has been good to us. A good thing too, because putting up with a dying person is difficult. If you love them, then it hurts you and them and if not, then they are just a nuisance.

when a man enters a woman, he does not hurt her if she does not have enough natural lubrication. It is also used to do what we are going to do when done between a man and a woman. So it is not unusual for a man to be carrying it." I smeared some on my fingers and reached around and found his tight hole. I rubbed my finger around and over his tiny puckered opening.

"Oh, that feels good." He was hooked already. He liked ass play. I just had to take it slow and easy. Then I pressed a finger gently, very gently against his hole and each time I pushed just a tiny, fractional amount to further open him up. I made sure that with each press I had rubbed my finger over some lubricant so that my finger was constantly getting wet again and would slide easily on the lubrication. Over and over I did this for about ten minutes. Each time going just a little bit further and several times putting more lubrication on my entire finger from the tube. Then on one try he opened up to me and my entire finger gained entrance to his inner most cavity. His secret spot.

When I had one finger inside of him, I just left it there and didn't move it. He jumped when I had entered him, but he didn't say anything. I just left it there and sucked on his dick a few times. Then, when he got hard again, I began to move my finger inside by bending my finger slowly and gently. I moved it around inside of him and I could feel a little hard spot inside of him just about where I would expect the end of his dick might be if it was that long inside of him. I could feel it pulse underneath my finger. I knew that this was that spot that Tobert liked to be stimulated. I very gently rubbed and stroked it softly. I continued this while is sucked on his dick.

"Oh, that feels good. What are you doing? And don't stop." I stopped sucking him and just continued rubbing him from the inside.

"Does that feel good?"

"How can you ask that? Look at me. I am leaking fluid and telling you not to stop. Of course it feels good. I don't know why, but it does. It feels wonderful. Why is that?"

"Because I am stimulating part of your sex system inside your body. I can do it and make love to you at the same time. Do you want me to try that with you." I wanted him to beg me to fuck him in so many words.

"Oh yes, yes, do it to me."

"It's called fucking you, and it may hurt a little at first, but this is how it will feel when you get used to me." I lubricated another finger and worked up to putting two fingers inside of him. When that second finger entered him, he jumped. "Did I hurt you?"

"No. It surprised me. And it hurts just a little. Like sometimes when I try to shit out something that seems too big. But it feels good too." He was at a loss for words momentarily. "I can't describe it. Is this all you do." I had to break it to him easy.

"No. But I will bet you are ready for the next step."

"Next step. What next step?" I kept rubbing him and then I bent my head down and again took him into my mouth. He was leaking fluid fast. I knew he was enjoying this immensely.

"I am going to put my love inside of you and continue to rub you with my love."

"You keep saying that, but what does that mean?"

"I am going to place my dick up your ass hole and rub you with my dick up there so that it will feel good to you." His eyes opened wide and he understood what I wanted to do to him. He started to tear up and cry.

"I have never done anything like that, and I never even thought about doing anything like that." He was scared. It was obvious. "I don't know if I want to do anything like that. I am afraid you will hurt me. What if I don't like it? What will you do?" I had to tell him the truth.

"It will hurt a little at first, but you feel how good my fingers feel up there, and how good my fingers are making you feel once I got them inside of you. It will feel better than that, and you will love it. Believe me, you will love it. You will want to do it over and over again."

"What if I don't? Will you stop?"

"I will if you give me 5 minutes before you make up your mind."

"What if I can't take five minutes."

"Well, the first five minutes, I won't even move and just let you get used to it. I won't move if it takes ten minutes. I won't move until you tell me to move."

"All right. Just. Please just don't hurt me." He was almost crying. I wouldn't hurt him deliberately. I put lubricant on my dick and some more on him. I had him lie on his stomach so that I could enter him while he was not strained. I reinserted my two fingers with some more lubrication and I kept up my digital intrusion into his body. I gradually inserted a third finger. Soon he was begging me to keep rubbing him.

"Lie very still and I will gradually enter you. Try not to fight me or squeeze down as then it may cause you more pain." I pressed the head of my dick to his opening and gradually applied a little pressure. He was still tight despite the three fingers that I had just removed from his hole. I told him to pretend he was taking a shit and he opened up a little and gradually just the initial part of the head of my dick gained entrance into his once forbidden territory. Then the complete head popped in past his muscle at the entrance to his ass hole, and I was in.

"Oh. My. Oh, that hurts." He whispered. Then he grimaced in obvious pain.

"Try to pretend you are taking a shit and gradually relax, and it won't hurt so much." He didn't do this. I could tell. After all, I had a very sensitive probe right there in his ass hole measuring how tense he actually was. I would know when he relaxed his hole, and its grip on anything, like me. I just kept completely still. I took the bottle and poured some lubrication directly on his ass hole as I held his cheeks apart. I pushed in a little and I could hear him sucking in his breath. I pushed most of the shaft of my dick into his hole and then I stopped. I pulled out a little and made sure more lubrication coated my dick and pushed into him again. Once I was seated almost completely inside of him, I laid down on top of him and held him and nibbled on his neck and then his ears.

"That feels good." He told me.

"In your ass hole?" I questioned.

"No, what you are doing to my neck and ears. My ass hole feels like it is on fire and hurts worse that anything I have ever felt before." How right he was.

"You are right that your ass hole is on fire; pretty soon you are going to beg me to start fucking you to put that fire out, and make you feel good."

"I sure hope you know what you are talking about because right now if you weren't laying on top of me I would have ripped your dick off and shoved it up your ass hole."

"Romantic aren't you." Well, at least I was in and had driven my point home. And I hadn't lied to him. I told him it would hurt. I just hoped it would also feel good to him as it should.

"Let me stick my dick up your ass hole and see how romantic

you are." Well, he was a feisty little thing, he was. I liked a challenge, but I didn't want to hurt him. I didn't like someone to just let me fuck them and yawn at the same time. I wanted to know they were receiving me and make me want to fuck the living shit out of them. I also wanted them to enjoy it. If I wanted an unemotional fuck, I could have had one of those new biosynthetic pussies. They even have them that look like an ass hole. You can buy them in the adult stores. Sure they cost a week's wages, but that was cheap for happiness and they folded up to something that could fit into a briefcase.

"I am going to start to move if that is all right."

"Yea get started, because then we are that much closer to getting finished." Oh he was going to be hard to break in. I started with short gentle little strokes inside of him. Gradually he loosened up a little. I could feel it.

"You are doing good now. Relax a little and pretend you are taking a dump and relax back here. I could tell he was trying and then suddenly he relaxed a lot and then I could gain complete and utter entrance into him without him fighting me.

"Awww." I could tell that he was now experiencing more pleasure. He was loose and I could move around in side of him more. The person getting fucked does not experience the greatest pleasure when getting fucked in this position. You have to have your dick hitting that spot inside of your partner and it is easier to hit it when they are turned such that the natural angle of fucking hits and rubs that spot on each stroke. I knew what I had to do next. I stopped momentarily and he spoke.

"Why did you stop, it was just beginning to feel good."

"It will feel even better. We are going to change positions."

"I don't think I could bear you taking it out and then putting it back in. It might hurt too much."

"Don't worry. I won't have to take it out."

"Then what are we going to do." I did have his attention.

"Just lie there. Do what I tell you, and you will see. First, we will roll over on your right side." He did that. "Now open your legs and let me turn to be between your legs." This is easier said than done. But with a little effort we accomplished it. As I did this, my dick rotated within him and he let out another Awwww. I know that this was not a pain sigh. I then had him lie back on his back. I had my dick up his hole and was kneeling on the sleeping platform between his legs. I then brought his bottom up to meet my body and I was again completely inside of him up to my balls. I waited a few moments for him to adjust. But he was ahead of me.

"Come on and fuck me. I want to feel you moving inside of me and making me feel good again." This was one hot little fucker. If everything worked out right, he was learning to love getting fucked.

"Here it comes. Get ready for that third leg I have."

"From the way it feels here, I think that may be an accurate description." He ohed and awed as I plowed into him over and over again in slow sensuous strokes designed to stimulate him to the maximum. The I leaned over and kissed him, and he fought for control of my mouth. He tried to suck my tongue down his throat. He chewed on my ears and tried to bite my neck and he told me he loved me and wanted to spend the rest of his life with me. I knew now. He was enjoying this position.

"Oh this is great. I want you to fuck me every night and every day. Oh, this feels wonderful. Fuck me harder. Oh, fuck me, fuck me. Fuck me more. Faster, harder, Do me." Man did he really get into this fucking. He loved to get fucked. He was another Tobert. And he was cute as could be. He was the cutest thing in four worlds that I had seen. Well okay, I hadn't been to four worlds yet, but I was willing to stake anything I found out there that he was the cutest thing around. As I look back upon it, he was. I didn't know at the time, that I would fall in love with someone. Nor did I know at the time that love is not a race always won by the cutest.

I didn't want to spoil his fun and cum too quickly. So I fucked and fucked him, for as long as I could. I really wanted him to enjoy this as long as possible. I did him slowly, then faster. I varied the pace. Most important of all, I moved around inside of him and changed the angle of the dangle as they say, and got all spots of the inside of him rubbed. Then I came back to that secret hidden spot that only guys know about, and hit it over and over again. I knew if I did it right he would have his own special pleasure.

"Oh. Oh. I think I am climaxing. What are you doing to me?"

"Nothing. I am just fucking you."

"Well, it feels great. Don't stop doing it. Yes. Oh yes, I can feel that I am going to cum."

"Well, don't hold back. Just tell me when you get there." I leaned over and chewed on his tits and kissed him again. Then his entire body tightened up and I could fell him jerk and pulsate underneath me. He tightened up his ass hole so tight, that I almost had to stop fucking him. That caused me to have my own climax. I pumped my seeds into him as he was shooting his on his chest. I bent over and licked his seed up and made sure he was clean. Then I leaned over again and kissed him.

"I couldn't tell you. It happened so quickly once it came upon me, and I couldn't control myself." He took his arms and hugged me while I was still inside of him. We kissed again and he held me close to him and began to cry.

"What's the matter? Did I hurt you?"

"No. You made me feel wonderful. At last I know that I am a man and that I truly love other men."

"And for that you are crying?"

"I am crying because I am no longer a virgin." He hesitated some more. "And I am crying because the man I love is you."

"Well, what's wrong with that?" I asked him, with a puzzled look on my face.

"When you get off the fiber transport, we may never see each other again."

"Is that all that is bothering you? We can fix that. Give me your personal pad." He handed me his personal communicator, and I entered my code into it and showed him my name and number. That would be able to locate me and deliver a message to me anywhere I could be found. It may take a few weeks, and if I am out of the system, then several months by hyper ship, but I would always be able to be located.[5] I handed him mine and he entered his identification number so that I could do the same. I was still inside of him. Then I questioned him. "I am still inside of you. Does it make you uncomfortable?"

"No. Not at all, it feels just right there. Where it belongs. I don't want you to ever take it out."

"Well, we would look pretty funny walking around with my dick stuck up you ass hole all day long. How would we explain it to

---

5   All messages, except local traffic, were converted to digital text messages and sent via stored memories in hyper ships which loaded the memories into the local ground facilities. Every time a ship went to the next sun, they had all communication records for you. This resulted in all messages eventually getting to their destination within about 10 days from the date sent for the longest destination. Usually a much shorter time than that, but the longer time was the published guarantee.

people?"

"I don't care. That is where it belongs."

"I agree with you. But this could pose problems, even if only when you try to eliminate wastes."

"I'll worry about that later." Was all he could say.

"Then you don't mind if I stay there a little longer, do you?"

"Not at all. Keep it there until we have to leave to get off at NES." I held him in my arms and faced him and let his legs go down some, but stayed inside of him. We kissed and I proceeded to give his upper body a complete tongue bath. I licked under his arms, his neck and his face. We kissed and then I chewed on his neck and I think I must have given him a slight bruise. His skin was lovely and soft, and his heart was willing for anything I could show him. His ears were particularly sensitive and even his nose liked my nibbles. I sucked on his tits, and he could not believe how wonderful it felt to have me sucking on his body, all parts of it. I worshiped his body for perhaps a half hour and by that time I was ready for another fuck.

"Are you sure you are not uncomfortable in this position?" I asked him again.

"No. I could live with your dick inside of me forever."

"I know that, but are your legs tired."

"I never thought about them." He hesitated as if considering it and replied, "No. Not if you are going to fuck me again. I like this position better than on my stomach. It feels better, and I get to see you and feel you and we can kiss."

"I know. It's my favorite position too."

"Are there others? Besides the two we have tried."

"Yes, many more. Just use your imagination. We could fuck while standing up."

"Why would you want to do that when we have a perfectly good sleeping platform right here?"

"Well, if we were in the shower together and let the water run down over our bodies while we fucked. It could be fun."

"Oh, I'm sorry you told me because now I will be looking for a shower large enough for the two of us. I want you to fuck me while I am showering."

"Well, perhaps we can find a place one day."

"But not today?"

"Not on this ship."

"Well, I guess you're right." About this time I was completely hard again. I moved around inside of him some more, and he smiled.

"Are you ready."

"Any time and all the time." I began the slow in and out movements that rubbed him. He smiled and I could tell he was already beginning to feel those feelings again. I took it slow, but I continued to fuck into and out of him for the next half hour. Several times I could feel his hole tighten up around me and I looked down and each time another drop of clear liquid oozed from his piss slit. Each time I leaned over and licked the head of his dick with my tongue I tasted his essence on my tongue. The little collection of fluid that pooled on his belly, I licked that up too.

"How is it feeling to you? Describe it for me."

"I don't know that I can. It is just such a different feeling that I don't know how to put it in words."

"Try anyway."

"Well, I can feel your big, and I mean very big dick inside of me moving all around. Not only is it long, it is big around, and that is what hurt me at first. But now, if you take if out, I would miss it and not feel complete. I can tell you where the head is because I think I can feel the head poking or at least rubbing me where it feels very good. And each time you poke me there or rub me there, something happens that makes my dick feel good. It is not like I am rubbing my dick. Similar to that, but not as hard. When you suck on my dick and take it into your mouth, it feels good, very good. I like that, but this rubbing you do is like scratching an itch I have that I can't reach myself. My only way out, my release, is my climax. Like the last time. You sucked my dick and finally that itch inside of me stopped itching for just a little time." We continued to fuck. I leaned over and kissed him some more and tried to force my tongue down to his stomach as gently as I could. With that long kiss, I felt his body tense up. Then I leaned over and took his dick in my mouth and sucked for all I was worth, trying to bring him to orgasm.

"Come on. Cum. Cum for me. Come on, cum you bastard." Well, I think that, but only a mumble comes out of my mouth with his dick in it. Then my lips make a hasty return around his dick. The intense efforts of my mouth and my staccato thrusts hitting that spot inside of him, did the trick. He started filling my mouth with his seed once again, and that caused me to spill my seed into him. I held him in my arms and we kissed again. I shared his seed with him, and we shared tongues for the longest time. When it was time for us to relax, I pulled out of him. I could see that he was visibly disappointed.

"Don't worry. I will enter you again in a few minutes." I turned him and we lay there on our sides, face to face. We kissed some more and I held him in my arms. "I think we need another rest." With that I closed my eyes and drifter off into the most contented sleep I had had in many months.

Chapter *Four*

We awoke about two hours later. He was nestled in my arms with his head against my chest. I held him closely and he looked up and kissed me. "Did you rest well."

"Of course. I was in your arms." I knew he meant it too.

"Tell me when you are up to more sex."

"How about now?"

"Are you sure."

"Of course I'm sure. I am also a little sore; so please be easy with me."

"You know I will." I turned him around and we lay side by side, but with his back to me. I held him again and then reached over and got the tube of lubrication. I put more on me. Then I very gently entered him again.

"That feels so good and now I don't feel empty like when I was sleeping." I held him to me and kissed his neck and caressed his head. Gradually I began to move inside of him. "Ohhhh. I can't believe how good that feels. Why is that so?"

"Because you are a man and a man has a special organ inside of him that feels good when another man enters him and fucks him."

"If that is so, then why don't all men like to get fucked as you call it? Why do men even waste their time with women?"

"Because not all men are attracted to other men. And then some of the men that are attracted to men, are afraid of the initial pain of having another man enter them. It is only the men who can stand the initial pain and have someone who is patient with them to teach them to accept a man within themselves. They have to want to give the man that enters them pleasure. Those people who want to share themselves and give their partner pleasure are truly lucky. With the right person, they feel the greatest pleasure, as you now know. The pleasure that equals that of fucking a woman. It can even exceed the pleasure of fucking and it can last much longer."

"It's amazing. I feel pleasure and all I have to do is lay here. I do not have to move. I can lie here and just let you worship my body and fill me full of your pursuit of your pleasure." He was almost panting as he said this.

"Yes, and if you tighten up your backside and hole, you can change the pleasure you feel and also increase the tightness around me and feel me more closely. Then you can relax, and let me fill you full of my pleasure. If you find that certain positions feel better to you, just tell me and guide me. I am here to pleasure you and to bring you to new heights of feelings. Just relax and let me fuck you into oblivion with this inner pleasure that you have learned to experience." With that he was putty in my arms. He relaxed even more, and I played with his body, licked his arms and pits and slobbered all over his face. I could tell that he loved it. I turned him enough to gently chew on his nipples and suck on his tits. He shook as I did this, and I could feel him tighten up his hole periodically and give me more pleasure. His body shook again, and I could tell that he was experiencing what the old books called an anal orgasm. More of his liquid flowed from his dick. It was clear. He shook several times and then he proclaimed he was cuming.

"I feel like I am climaxing, over and over again. Yet none of my seed is exiting my body, and I am still hard. My seed feels like it is spewing forth as I speak. Yet I can see that no seed is exiting me. What is happening to me?"

"You are having an anal orgasm. It is when a man gets fucked and climaxes without cuming. You can do this over and over again if you are patient. This is what happens to a woman when a man fucks her and she cums more than one time. With the right person, this can go on for a long time. Are you enjoying yourself?"

"Of course I am. And as you say, it is because you are the right man." We continued to be locked dick in ass for the next few hours. I would slow down and rest and allow him to rest while I stayed inside of him. At the same time, I rested and held back my climax. I do not know how many times he tightened up while I fucked him over the next few hours, but I know that he was enjoying himself immensely as he turned around several times, grabbed my head and tried to suck my tongue down his throat. Then, he licked and chewed my face, my ears and my upper body that he could reach. Over and over again I brought him to anal orgasms and felt him tighten up upon me. The last time, I decided to get my nut (old world slang for climax) and allowed myself to cum. Once I had my climax, he stated he could feel me pumping myself into him. We rested in that position. When we awoke, I began fucking him anew.

"I don't ever want you to leave my ass hole. You belong there inside of me. I want you there for the rest of my life. Marry me. I am of age. Marry me and live with me. I will support you. You need never work again in your life." He proposed to me. I was flattered.

"I can't marry you. I joined the space corps and have a tour of duty to perform."

"Well then, I will marry you and live with you."

"What will your parents say? You said that you didn't want to tell them you preferred men. They wanted grandchildren."

"At this point, I don't care what they think. I love you and want to marry you."

"After only 8 hours of a honeymoon and without the benefit of clergy? How can you love me, you don't even know who I am. You don't even know me well enough to like me, let alone to marry me." He looked crestfallen, actually depressed.

"I love you. I know I love you. I want to marry you." He looked up at me. "What do you find so hard to believe?"

"I will make a deal with you. My tour of duty is over in five years. We can see each other as often as our schedules permit. If after that time, if then you still want to marry me, and you still have not meet anyone, then, we can talk about marriage." By the time that five years has gone by, he will be as old as me and have had a succession of lovers and forgotten all about me. "By that time you will be as old as I am now. Twenty years old is not old enough to be an old maid."

"What's an old maid?"

"Sorry, another old world slang term. It meant a girl who had not married and waited for the right man until she was very old. She was still a virgin, a maiden, but she was old. The term meant some older woman who was waiting for her prince charming and he had never come. Back then that was a woman who was perhaps 40 or more years old and never married."

"That's old not to have been married. Practically one fourth of their life gone."

"No, back then people only lived until they were 30 or forty and even the oldest people only lived until 60 or 70 years old. Oh, some lived longer, but very few."

"You're kidding me, aren't you."

"No, you didn't pay attention in history class did you."

"Well, it was rather boring and it didn't seem to apply to us. That happened so long ago."

"Well, you should have listened. It's the way we were back then."

"You were a history major and went into the space corps?"

"No, I just like to read a lot."

"About stuff that is boring. Not near as interesting as reading about sex."

"You don't read between the lines. All mankind's history is about sex. Everything man ever did is about wealth, power and sex. The easiest way to power and money is to marry it. That is, have sex with the person with money or power and you instantly marry into money. Back in those days, power meant money in other forms. You have only known me for about 8 hours, and already are offering me money to marry you and live comfortably for the rest of my life."

"Well, I know that you are not greedy, or you would have married me for money and to let me support you."

"Wrong you are, penis breath, and dick in ass hole boy."

"Why am I wrong?"

"I don't need your money."

"You think the space corps pays well enough to support you in the style I would like you to be accustomed?"

"No, but the money I inherited from my great-great-grandparents allows me to be comfortable and can supplement what I earn and that is enough for me to live comfortably. I don't need money to be happy." I need not tell him I could probably buy and sell him and his family three times over. Just enough to let him know that I am immune to money inducements so he will stop trying to buy my devotion. As to his sweet little ass being the bait, he could catch me any time, any place without any other inducements.

However, my present inducement was my hard dick inside his ass hole and it was a relly good inducement right now. It was feeling really good to me. I had momentarily slowed down fucking him while we had this conversation, and I again began fucking him with a regular motion. I knew I could get him to experience a few more climaxes if I worked his body right. We fucked on and off for the next four hours and several times he moaned out my name and clawed at the coverings on the sleeping platform. He was experiencing pleasure as he had never know it before today.

When my pad alarm rang to signal that we only had an hour left before we would have to report to the lounge, I woke up John by resuming my fucking motion. He turned toward me and kissed me. "Good morning lover." He told me. "Is the honeymoon over?"

"Almost." I told him. "We have just an hour to finish up and to get out to the lounge to get our seats before they send someone to come and find us. I am sure you don't want them to find us still locked in a fucking embrace where they have to pry us apart."

"Why not. It certainly would save on having to explain anything to my parents."

"You think. I think not."

"You worry too much."

"You don't worry enough."

"I told you. I can support the two of us."

"And what do you do at the ripe old age of 18. Brain surgery, better than any computer can perform it. I think not. Just be satisfied that I want to see you again and will do my best to fuck that pretty little ass of yours any chance I can get. In the mean time, just keep it greased and ready for me. Is that a deal?" I knew he meant well, but his wants were unrealistic. Even if his family had money, it wasn't likely that they had more than my family. Similar to my family, they wouldn't turn it over to their son and his male lover. Sure we could get married and with the property laws, unless he was killed in an accident, all of his money would stay in his family unless he left a portion to me. Even then, he could only leave a portion, less than half to me. The rest went to his children if he had any, and if he didn't it went back to his parents or his siblings. If nothing else, in default of family and siblings, then it went to the government. He just didn't understand. "Just hang on as I intend to fuck your ass right into the next sleeping compartment. Are you up to it?"

"I am if you are man enough to put it to me and fuck me better than you have done up until now."

"Trying to complain about the fucking service now that you have already received the goods and want to renege on the deal. (Sorry old world slang for back out of the deal.) Your ass hole and your precious body are mine to command. Any time and any place I want.

"Promises, promises. But I am impressed, your called my body precious. You must really like it then."

"No, I corrected. I like you, but your hole is just a hole, like any other hole. Filled with nothing."

"No." He corrected. "Filled with one of the biggest, most conceited pieces of male flesh I have ever had the misfortune to meet and fall in love with. You won't marry me and make me an honest woman. For that is what I am, nothing more than your woman with a hole for her man to fuck."

"Stop talking like that. I hate that. You are not a woman, and don't act like one. You are a guy, a man. Act like one. I like guys, men, not women. If you start acting like a woman, no man who likes men will want you. You will be ridiculed and find no acceptance anywhere. However, if you act like a man, then it does not matter and is of no concern to anyone who you choose to take to your bed. Remember that. You can't help who you love, but you can choose how you act. Don't act to bring scorn and ridicule upon yourself." He had hit a sore spot with me. I had been approached by several men seeking other men, but they acted like women. That turned me off. Some were attractive, but once they opened their mouths and acted like a woman, I lost any and all interest in them. I am not prejudice. I can't be. After all, I am attracted to men. I like to stick my dick in their mouths and up inside their ass holes. I can't be prejudice against other men who like to do the same thing. But I am not turned on by women or anyone who acts like a woman. Don't get me wrong. I like women, just not in a sexual way. I do not feel any sexual attraction for them.

The really cute men like John, I will take their dicks in my mouth and blow them while they blow me. I will swallow their seeds and drink them down. I want a guy, a man, not a woman with a dick.

We fucked for the rest of the hour and I got him to climax without spilling his seed several times. For my climax, I turned him around again and faced him while we made love. We kissed and embraced while I sucked him and pumped my final load into him. Again and again I rammed it home inside of him. When finally, I could fuck no more, I leaned over and finished his blow job. He filled my mouth with his seed and we were both spent beyond belief.

Then I held his legs up and sucked on his ass hole. I told him this would ease his soreness and he could squeeze himself if he could, and feed me all of my seed that I had pumped into him in the last 12 hours.

"Oh that feels good on my abused ass hole. I can't believe that you fucked me for more than 12 hours. I feel like my hole has been flooded with your sperm and they are leaking out of me."

"Perhaps they will if you don't let me suck them from your hole right now. I can't let you go back to your parents with this now rather large opening in your back side that won't close and is leaking all this white, man seed. Let me suck it out of you and soothe your tired pucker with my warm moist tongue."

"Agreed. That sounds so good to me right now." He rolled over onto his stomach and held his rear end up in the air just a little to give me easier access. "Kiss it and make it better." He told me. "Suck me dry and let me rest in peace. I may never walk right again, thinking that I have a third leg still implanted up there." I licked and sucked for about twenty minutes while he forced as much of my seed out of his hole as he could. I then slapped his ass and told him we had ten minutes to get dressed. We both scrambled to get our clothes on, and then I let him leave first. I picked up my belongings including my camera and the two satellite units for our true holographic record of this marathon event. I packed up my belongings and got ready to walk out of the sleeping unit. I was just a minute or two behind John. I heard his parents greeting him and tell him they were glad to see him. He told them that he had rented a sleeping unit and rested during the trip. They were glad that he was not bored with the trip. They wondered if he had practiced any while he was in his room. He told them, no, he was working on a new arrangement. I didn't understand what he meant.

We all moved to the two lounges and had secured ourselves when the twenty minute warning buzzer sounded and the rest of the passengers all collected in the two lounges. I was seated where I could see John and he could see me. We smiled at each other, but other wise never said a word.

Chapter *Five*

The docking procedure at the Fiber Station was what they had taught us in school. We had felt the decrease in gravity as we traveled up from the Earth. We were strapped in our seats in the lounge. Our magnetic boots keep our feet firmly on the deck until we had gotten to our sleeping quarters. When we came to the station, our double lounge car was unhooked and we floated free. I know that some of the passengers might have thought that we came unhooked and floated free into space. The warning announcement had informed us that we might experience momentary weightlessness and some discomfort, but that it would pass as our compartment would be place under artificial gravity. Actually, it took much longer than I expected. We were in free fall[6] for probably about 30 seconds to a minute. I was glad that I had not eaten anything in the last few hours.

---

6   The correct term is free fall or sometimes freefall. To the non space man, just think of it as a weightless condition. When orbiting the earth or any planetary body with gravity, a body in motion circling or orbiting the planet is actually falling toward the planet and so is the ship you are riding in. However, because the motion of the ship is also around the planet the velocity or speed of the ship is to fall over the horizon of the planet. The effect is actually that of having little or no perceptible weight whatsoever. You are actually falling and traveling around the planet at the same time. Some people call this zero gravity, but it is not. For instance the actual force of the gravity of the earth is not eliminated as you travel away from the earth. At an altitude of about 100 km (62+ miles) the pull of the earth's gravity is about 97% of the force at sea level. You feel your own weight when standing on the surface of the earth because the earth is resisting your movement in its gravitational field. That attraction is toward the center of the earth. Satellites and other orbiting bodies stay in space their tremendous horizontal speed to circle the earth is somewhat balanced by the pull on them toward the Earth by the gravity of the Earth. Thus, the ground's curved withdrawal along the Earth's round surface offsets the satellites' fall toward the ground.

Several of the passengers I could swear turned green and held their sickness bags in front of their faces. John grinned at me. We could feel the compartment unhooking from the lower sleeping compartments and then our two lounge compartments together traveled to a receiving area and passenger disembarkment terminal. The Fiber Station is deceiving. For security reasons and also just for practical reasons, the actual station is composed of about a dozen stations. The Fiber terminus is actually a counter balance, a weight and the computer brains which can travel up and down the terminal end of the fiber by several thousand meters to change the balance, the load, the unloading and loading areas, and all the factors they need to regulate and service the fiber itself. Below the terminus are the docking ports composed of many orbiting stations. Most are for cargo and for the storage of cargo compartments and containers until the proper ship arrives to pick them up.

All of the cargo stations can accept passengers, but only two of the stations are set up for passengers to stay any length of time. We were quickly ferried off to our assignments, and there I lost sight of John. He waived good bye and he was gone. I was met on the station by my ferry captain who would bring me to DES. I could shag a ride and not have to be treated like a passenger. They just told me to sit in the extra seat in the pilot's compartment and not to touch anything or they would space me. Actually, they wouldn't have to space me. If I touched the wrong thing, it could send us into the Sun, very unlikely, but most likely off into outer space not to be rescued before we ran out of air. These ferry boats don't carry a lot of reserve air. Air not needed. Wasted mass used to carry around unnecessary air mass. Wasted energy expended lugging around unnecessary air mass. Hey, air has mass. Who wants to pay to haul around more than you need plus a reasonable safety precaution. Oh, we had reserves, but not enough for a crew of three people and perhaps forty passengers.

They told me we were full of mostly cargo, so we had reserves for three, now four people for a few weeks. If I wasted it, I would still be the only casualty on an otherwise routine trip. These people didn't kid around. No sense of humor when it came to the safety of the ship or their lives. The trip was unremarkable. For me it was exciting. I strapped myself in and felt a small boast for about a minute and then we coasted for an hour or two. I felt the ship turn once or twice with a short push for mid course corrections. Later we had a few blasts and then a deceleration of about a minute. Then we bumped slightly and the magnetic locks clicked and the board in front of the pilot had a bunch of green lights flash and she unstrapped. Did I forget to mention that the pilot was a woman. She was beautiful, for a woman. She had her hair cut short, about an inch or two as is common with women in space. This was especially true of working women such as pilots, professional women, doctors, nurses, engineers, etc. Long hair got in the way of working people especially in zero and low gravity (lo g) situations. I was probably the first of any of my fellow passengers to arrive at DES.

DES was in an orbit that just barely qualified it to be a space station circling Earth. It was perhaps just short of the half way point to the moon. The next station was Moon Station (called Mo Stat or just Mo by the locals) and appeared as if it circled the Moon and not the Earth. It had an orbit period that equaled the revolution of the Moon around the earth. In this fashion, it was always over the same spot relative to the moon and it appeared to be standing still if you were on the surface of the moon. From the Earth, the station revolved around the earth every 28 days, one lunar month. Therefore, the station was always moving and yet appeared to be standing still. We didn't need a Carbon Fiber Stalk to the moon. We didn't ship that much stuff from the moon such that we would save money on building a stalk. The gravity wasn't that strong that we had to expend tremendous amounts of energy to overcome its gravity. We needed it for earth to overcome the earth's gravity to put things into space. However, to send things to the earth, we just had to drop them into the gravity well for them to land on the earth. The trick was to keep them from burning up on the way down. On the moon they didn't burn up, no air. You just had to be careful not to be Dorothy and drop something on somebody. Dorothy was a character in an old earth story about someone who dropped her house on some witch or somebody. And before you ask, no! I don't know how she got her house into space to drop it on anybody or why it didn't burn up on reentry.

I wasn't assigned quarters because my assignment would be on the milk run ship and that was where I would live. While on DES, I would be allowed access to temporary transient lodgings on an as needed, and as available basis. It was just possible that I would be on DES and not have a place to sleep for hours on end. I could live with that as I always hoped I could hook up with someone and spend some quality time with them. I didn't need to sleep, just a place to park my private parts for a few hours. Or more preferably, a person in which to park my private parts for mutual fun and no games.

On DES they fed me, allowed me to freshen up and gave me a berthing assignment on the Galileo XII. The 12th ship of that name to be commissioned, that makes the Ganymede run. Tradition had it that the ship making the regular Ganymede run was always named Galileo. I was told to report to the ship within two hours. I just had enough time to become somewhat familiar with DES layout and then report for duty. The station is of course somewhat circular. The original space stations were not circular. Yes, all of the original science fiction stories from the old libraries had big orbital space stations that spun in space and created artificial gravity through rotation. They were supposed to be large circular things where you could start walking in one direction and eventually walk completely around and return to your starting point. It doesn't work that way in real life. Sorry folks, reality doesn't even suck. If it did there would be more of us having a lot more fun than some of these up tight people deserve. The early stations were not large enough to be large doughnut shapes. DES was built or assembled in space and took over 50 years to complete. It started as the smaller inner rings and grew and grew. As they needed more room and facilities, they added rings. The rings were like levels of construction, but not doughnut rings. From space it looked more like a relatively flat waffle with irregular spots, gaps and clumps. They were not aesthetically pretty, but extremely functional.

We now have minimum artificial gravity that adds to the gravity produced by centrifugal force to be almost Earth normal or one gravity in the outer areas of DES. In this manor, all the "rings" of the station have some gravity and the inner ones can have that gravity turned on and off. The inner most rings are reserved for zero gravity laboratories where any trace of gravity is destructive of the purpose of the research. I got to see the highlights of the station by visiting a few levels. I did manage to see a bar I wanted to catch the next time I came through. I am not much of a drinker, but I find that a little liquid refreshment dulls the senses, eases the psychological pain of first man sex and first entry. It also fogs the brain to what you actually consented to in the initial stages of seduction. It also eases the pangs of regret of first entry. Love and sex shouldn't always be a pain in the ass. It has got to go in the ass, but it shouldn't always be a pain in the ass even the first time. Alcohol helps alleviate the pain. It also keeps you from getting punched out sometimes too. I didn't have any experience, but always thought about planning ahead. I was not going to wear an M-M badge or symbol in a bar like this. I could find a willing soul, or ass hole, without declaring my purpose to everyone in the bar.

While it is not illegal or forbidden to engage in man-man sex, there are still some provincial individuals who think that you are insulting their manhood to proposition them for sex. Propositioning someone for sex is a compliment, not an insult. You like someone enough to want to be with them physically. That is not an insult. But when the recipient is a man, unless you have big tits, they don't always take it the right way, as a compliment. The local constabulary don't always enforce the law as it was intended. Many a man has fallen down a flight of stairs at a bar after making a sexual pass at another man. And this, in a bar without a set of stairs.

The Galileo XII, called the Galo 12, the "Gal" or "Old Gal" by the crew, was a nice ship. I had ample quarters that I shared with about 20 other young men of various ages. We shared both our living and sleeping quarters. We each had our own assigned sleeping platform that was ours. We could go there anytime we were not on duty. The living quarters had a nice lounge area for watching TV, playing cards, writing messages and just doing nothing. It had artificial gravity to keep us in our bunks and on the deck plates. The gravity was about 1/3 Earth standard. This was just enough gravity to keep us comfortable. The working areas of the ship had about half Earth normal gravity that pulsated. The pulsation effect we couldn't feel, but it used less power and actually caused our bodies to react as if physiologically as if we were about ¾ earth standard gravity or slightly more. We had to keep up our fitness and too little gravity would allow the deterioration of our bones and body. As it was, we still had to take our supplements and exercise almost each day in the high G gymnasium, called the G gym. Only an hour each day kept the doctor away they used to say. We had lots of hot water to wash with because we distilled our own from our own waste water. We had a full complement of men, about 2,000 including all the various specialties. From multiple doctors, specialists, scientists and the like, we had them all. However, most of us, about 1,800 of us, were Space Corps members used for handling, transporting cargo, persons, scientific supplies and the like.

While I was billeted in enlisted men's quarters, I was on the road for fast promotion. As soon as I completed my first tour of duty as an intern and became familiar with all the jobs in my skill line, I would be rotated back to the academy for more training and eventually promoted above these corps members. Many had joined as young as age 18 right out of trade school. Some even younger had worked on the ground and then at age 18 requested off world assignments and spent an additional 2 years in specialized training on Earth. There was nobody who worked off world who was not at least 17 years of age. Some things still required the maturity that only age can bring. Also, unless there was some reason to send a non physically mature worker into less than earth standard gravity, they just didn't do it. The work was hard, but not that hard strength wise. The human body had evolved to thrive in earth's gravity and developed best according to plan under 1 earth standard gravity. While everything was done by machines, nothing weighed what it did on Earth. But it still had the same mass. The machines needed a steady hand and an experienced brain to operate them. Sure, you could be an idiot and do the job, but the computer controls just worked better with an intelligent live hand to supervise them. There were very few accidents with injuries and even fewer fatal accidents. But there were always some accidents, and this the captain and the crew always liked to kept to a minimum. Mostly they were minor things, but there were some fatalities in space even to this day. The Gal had a very clean record. No crew fatalities that were no attributed to any, but unavoidable situations. The Galo had absolutely no crew errors in 14 standard years since her commission. An unblemished record and we intended to keep it that way. We did not even have a machine error on our record yet.

Some of the men were married and had wives on Earth or at DES or on the Moon. Some were registered M-M couples and they lived and berthed separately. Not discrimination, just a hold over of separating the sexes so that the married men and opposite sexes (and I guess temptation) were not present while you slept. Anyone was free to have whatever sexual relations they wished in private. However, your sleeping quarters were not private. A few of the men were married to each other and they were given married quarters. I saw a few of them in passing and they appeared to be very happy together. I didn't know any or work with any of them. I just wasn't ready to declare myself, and probably wouldn't be ready for at least another 100 years. I figured after I reached 100, if people hadn't figured it out by then, they probably never would. Of course, then I would be spared the trouble of explaining it to them.

I saw the man flesh that I was rooming with and they all were between the ages of 17 and 30. Most were young, but there was a group of men who were around 25, and this pleased me to no end. I liked the mature bodies of the 22 to 25 year old men and the pretty soft bodies of the 17 year old men. I liked the bodies of all of them to tell you the truth. I even liked the ones in between my favorite ages. I liked the bodies of the mature 25 and a few 30 year old guys I saw in my quarters and in the rest of the ship. I have to confess; I just liked guys. In the gym, you got to see just about everyone in the raw. You saw them in the raw in the showers and changing rooms. The exercise microsuits left nothing to the imagination. You could practically count the number of pubic hairs a man had through the suits. All exercises were conducted wearing only a jockstrap and a skin tight micro-fiber suit which adsorbed the perspiration. They were only as thick as the thinnest sheet of paper, but hugged you like a second skin. It left nothing to the imagination. You would think that it would be better to wear nothing but the jock strap, but you needed the suit to adsorb the perspiration and not let it go flying off into the air. There was a special air filtration system that warmed the air to the optimum temperature and dried it for the moisture content in the G gym. The result was the ship recaptured all the sweat. The suits were deposited for processing after workouts. They were not disposable, but washed to get the minerals out and then evaporated and sterilized in a vacuum. Remember, no germs survive in a vacuum. They had perfected vacuum virus sanitation over 100 years ago. All oils turn to a crust that is quickly blown or sucked away as a powder which can also be harvested. All a part of the ship's normal routine to process the uniforms. The fiber stretches and so just three or four sizes fits everyone, just about.

The ship is built not like the gleaming rocket ships of long ago, but more like an ocean liner. Since they were assembled in space and don't have to travel through an atmosphere, being aerodynamic is not necessary. The ships are sleek and look something like an irregularly shaped fat hot dog with the bun. The front is somewhat pointed and the ship is long so that we do not set up too much drag if we have to move in the solar winds. We also don't want large things hanging off from the sides to come loose. Remember, no weight does not mean no mass. If you study the Galo and her sister class ships that travel to other suns, you will find that up close she had lots of hand holds, antenna, openings, and other anomalies which would cause someone to question if the people who designed her knew what they were doing; and if the people who built her followed the plans. Well, they all knew what they were doing and therefore she looks exactly like she should.

I will tell you more as we get into my tale, but this is enough for you to get an idea. The decks were labeled from the front of the ship to the back. The front always started with alpha deck. The last deck was always omega deck. This came from the old hold over of using the Greek alphabet to label things. This caused some problems as there were only 24 letters in the Greek alphabet and some ships didn't have 24 decks and some had more than 24 decks. Thus we got the bastard nomenclature of alpha deck, alpha-1, alpha-2, beta-1, and beta-2 decks. Each ship had its own nomenclature. You had to learn it. But knowing the deck's name gave you a rough idea where it was located in the ship. The middle of the ship was always the dividing line and when you named the decks from the rear, you counted from the rear. The rear deck was always omega.

If a ship had less than 24 decks, then you left out some of the middle letters and for more decks you used all the letters and added numbers to make up the difference. You numbered from 1 to 9. Usually you didn't get past about 4 numbers. This was because no ship had more than 100 decks. That is 24x4 different names. Even the Galo had less than 50 decks. Of course some of these decks were huge as they were giant cargo holds that would easily qualify as the size of four normal decks. However, since they were accessed as one deck, they only had one name. Theta deck didn't have a 1, 2, 3 or 4. It was just theta deck. I had learned the symbols for the Greek alphabet in school. I was at home on the ship once I got used to actually using what I had learned. What I did spend lots of time trying to figure out was scouting out places where I could be alone with someone. You know, good places to fuck a friend. I knew where to fuck them. I meant a good place on the ship to accomplish the deed without witnesses or prying eyes. Most ships had visual monitors through out the ship, and your personal communications badge, which was also your ID badge, could trace your movements anywhere on the ship and reported when you left the ship.

The brass, our name for the high officers that ran the ship, usually never queried the ship to locate anyone or tell them who was with anyone. You got very little privacy on the ship in your shared quarters, and so if you could find some of your own, they didn't want to disturb you. Unless, and this was a big unless, you were not where you were supposed to be at the time of your duty schedule. If you were fucking your brains out, then you would be a happier corps member and more inclined to stay were you were assigned and doing your job and not making waves as the expression goes. Don't ask, don't tell and if I know, let me forget about it. Just don't force me to have to do anything about it. As a practical matter, you were free to fuck anything that consented on your own tine. Just don't do it in the public corridors. Don't fuck with married people because it was bad for morale. If you were a M-M, then wear your badge and you were free to proposition anyone. The worst he could do is turn you down. If he reported you, he would be reprimanded, not you. Without the badge you would be written up and told to wear your symbol. Then anyone who spoke to you knew the score. Married people were off base because if you were married you were secure in the knowledge that your spouse, be they man or woman, was not off fooling around with anyone while you were on duty. They also usually set up the duty rosters for married couples to maximize their off duty times together. This was good for morale or good old fashioned immorality within a marriage. I say this because many religions used to consider sex even within marriage not moral unless it was for the purpose of procreation, having children. How niave and rediculous can you get? I don't even want to think about that line of absurd thought. Fucked out happy people make for a happy crew and they don't have the energy or the inclination to get into trouble. That is trouble with a capital S E X. Remember, sex is a basic instinct like eating. We serve you three meals a day and snacks if you need or want them. You have to find your own sex, but if you can fit it in three times a day, more power to you.

I immediately found about a half dozen places to be alone with someone. Next task was to find the person to be alone with. That was a little harder. There were jokes about the men in M-M (Man-Men) quarters who fooled around and stepped out on their friends or lovers, but I didn't believe it. Like I said, it is bad for morale. I think those rumors were started just to break the ice to see who wanted to play around. The married M-M's mixed with us for work, but were really happily married and nobody fucked with them sexually or even bothered them with jokes or anything. They seemed like good guys that just happened to be married to another guy. But the scoop was that the single M-M's might just take care of any willing M-W fellow who let them know he wanted to be serviced. This didn't help me. I didn't want a blow job or to be serviced. I liked fucking little boy's ass holes. Please note the term little boy means anyone younger than me. I didn't want a child nor anyone under the age of consent. I really didn't want any one who was not mature enough to love me back as an equal. Well maybe John was an exception, but he actually was very mature for someone so young. I craved the kind of ass holes that were attached to boys and men who had not had half the space corps up their holes. I wasn't afraid of disease. We had finally conquered all known social diseases and constantly monitored for new ones. We had not found one in the last 85 years. I wasn't even concerned with finding an ass hole that had been reamed out by so many men that it wasn't tight enough.

I was concerned with my pride and ego. I wanted someone who wanted me. Not just someone who wanted a big dick or a dick to fuck them. I wanted to be wanted and needed as me, a person. I didn't want to be tossed away with the old laundry. Oh, I wasn't ready to settle down, but I didn't want someone who, when I finished and was drawing out my dick, who yelled next over his shoulder. I still had a little pride. Maybe not much, but I still had a little. Sex should be interesting, not just a testing to see if the hole was still open for business. I wasn't looking for everlasting love just yet, but I was looking for some meaning in the act. Even if the only attraction was that, I just liked the person at first. Maybe I am reading too much into this sex stuff and trying to put meaning into it that really isn't there. Time will tell or I will get over it.

I had been on the Galo for about a week when I got a message from John. It was short and sweet. He had settled in and was living with his parents on DES waiting for his father's transfer to the moon. If I was ever in the neighborhood, please let him know and we could take up our last visit where we left off. I sent him a message and told him I was on the Galo 12 and that I would be back in about a lunar (a month) and when the berthing schedule with DES was posted, I would let him know. We could take in a movie and get reacquainted.

One of the next best things that happened was my bunk mate, Gert. He was of German ancestry and had the most beautiful blue eyes and blond hair. He didn't look real. He was so pretty. He was also older. He never talked about any girlfriend or about how many girls back home on Earth he had banged the shit out of or anything. He usually stared at me during exercise time and we shared a steam bath cleaning once and then showered in the common showers. I think I saw his dick getting hard a few times. Of course to my credit, many guys stared at me because I was larger than most of them. Many just had natural curiosity, but some were really interested. I had to be careful in determining which category Gert fell into.

I decided to make my move. One shift after work, I asked him if he had seen the movie that was playing that week. I always preferred to see a movie the first time, especially the action ones, on a large screen. He said he hadn't and I asked him if we could go together as I had not seen it. I told him I didn't know too many people yet and didn't want the guys to think I was stuck up or too good for them. I assured him I was friendly, but didn't know too many of them. They had had several runs together and some had years to get to know each other.

We had finished up our shift, gone to the G gym and worked out together and then taken a steam and shower together. He got mostly hard during the shower, but neither of us said a word. I let myself get a partial erection too and then we rinsed off and got dressed. We went to the movie in compartment 37 on zeta deck. The room is rather large. It seats about 200 people in rows that were slanted back so that each row behind you was slightly elevated and everyone had a good view of the large screen. We sat and watched the movie and had a good time. We each had an alcoholic drink, we were off duty and the automated bartender kept track of our personal codes so that neither of us could have more than two drinks. The last drink had to be more than 8 hours before our next shift. The ship left nothing to chance. The ship wanted us to be happy, but in good working order for our next duty shift. Ours would be tomorrow for both Gert and me.

I wasn't worried. Before reporting for work you always had to show your arm ID to punch in for the record. I knew that the machine could measure your blood for alcohol and other chemicals to see that all workers were fit for duty. The light and wave scanners could detect substances without penetrating the skin. If there was any doubt, then a more detailed analysis could be requested. I had never heard of one being requested. Everyone had the best interest of the ship at heart. If anyone messed up, it affected us all. In space that meant that your life depended on the man next to you doing his job. Doing his job properly, efficiently, on time, and without an error of any kind whatsoever. Check, double check and recheck anything and everything. You only made a mistake once. Then, if you were still alive and your ship in one piece, you were shipped back home. After the show, we were feeling great as the drinks were good and they relaxed us and made the mood more festive. We talked for a while and he wanted to show me the aft-star room. As an astronomer, he had access to the aft-star room and knew that I might find it interesting. We were headed out from our orbit, and the forward star room was in constant use. The aft one would not normally be in use unless needed. This would give him the opportunity to show me around and what he does as part of his job. We headed for the room and passed several people we knew in the passage ways. We stopped and had a brief chat, and then moved on. I was getting edgy and impatient to be alone with him, and I sensed so was he.

When we arrived, we entered the compartment and checked the schedule. No one was scheduled to use the room for another 8 hours. The compartment is not the star room. The actual star room is the last ten feet of the other side, the outer ship side, of the next air tight room. The star room was next to the outer skin of the ship. The ship and the room are shielded against air leaks and other hazards. You didn't have heavy lead shielding because that would set up a cascade effect of radiation that would kill everyone in the ship. Most cosmic radiation travels through us and the ship without harming us. That is because there isn't a lot of radiation. If there is, you are dead anyway. We are, just like most matter, mostly empty space. We can generate a magnetic field enough to repel most radiation if needed, even in periods of higher than normal radiation. We can't shield against everything. Not even an entire planet the size of the earth can effectively shield the surface of the earth from mega bursts of gamma radiation. Anyway the star room is the next compartmentalized room out from the entrance chamber. You can only enter it through a round circular port that you climb up through on a ladder and close the hatch. The outer shell of the ship is actually transparent there, and you can retract the outer covering and directly view the stars. The room is only about ten feet tall, but you can see almost one half of the entire universe from there. The other half is hidden by the ship. I had read about it and seen pictures of it, but if you have never seen it in person, it defies description.

We entered the anteroom and then dimmed the lights so that our eyes could get used to the reduced lighting conditions. Gert lead me to the entrance hole and climbed the stairs and opened the round port. We climbed up the access ladder and he closed the hatch to secure it against an air leak if the ship was struck with a meteorite while the protective shutters were open. He also illuminated the warning light that told others entering the room that others were already in the star chamber and the protective shutters were being opened. We stood there in the dark for a while and let our eyes adjust. Gert explained all this to me. All this time he held on to me while we were alone in the dark. He told me just a little longer. I could feel his body next to mine and he brushed up against me. I could feel his hard dick against my body. I accidentally rubbed my hand over his hardness and he did the same to me.

Well, that was all it took. I could not see him but I could feel him and our lips met and we kissed. He was an older man. My first older man and he kissed like he had had some experience at this. I grant you, age 25 was not that old, but a mature man knows what he wants and is not too bashful in letting you know what he wants. Our tongues did a mock battle for supremacy of our mouths. I think I won, and soon he was sucking my tongue down his throat. We kissed, then his lips moved on and he made love to my neck, face and upper body with his hands and then his mouth. We quickly stripped off our clothing and we both stood there stark naked, not that either of us could see the other. We didn't need lights, we could feel each other and that was enough.

I had thoughtfully brought some lubrication in the pocket of my coveralls. Gert fell to his knees and took the head of my dick into his mouth. He must have had lots of practice doing this; because within about four or five up and down movements, he had taken my entire length into his mouth and down his throat. I had never before had anyone who could take all of me in their throat. This was both amazing and wonderful. I was in awe of his oral skills that he could get all of me inside of his mouth and down his throat without choking. We lay down on the flooring and found a patch of carpeting where we could rest. Carpeting is very rare in space, as it just gets dirty, can not be easily cleaned and does not allow the boots to grip magnetically. However, in the star chamber, it keeps down the noise, no sparks to create static electricity with the special fibers of the antimagnetic carpeting and the machinery will not magnetically stick to the deck such that it can not be easily repositioned. There are strips of it on the floor for convenience. There were also strips of bare deck where the machinery once positioned could be magnetically secured. We found a strip of carpeting. There is nothing colder than a strip of bare decking on naked flesh, ass being particularly sensitive.

I then connected with his dick and found that he too had the plaything of a man and not that of a boy. He was at least 18 cm and a nice size around. He too had his foreskin intact and did not belong to a religion that mandated the removal of the foreskin. The government could not prohibit it if the practice was for religious purposes, but many times even within that religion, they opted for the man to make that decision once he reached the age of consent of 16 or 17. I had not had a dick in my mouth since I was with John on the ride up on the beanstalk. That was already more than two weeks in the past. I was so horny; I would have sucked a stick at this point. Or at least a big stick. Gert was ready and so was I. We worked each other's dicks around in our mouths and I could feel him tightening up. He pumped a good load of his seed into my mouth. That excited me to no end, and thus I quickly hit my psychological trigger and then shot a load of my seed into Gert's mouth. I could feel him sucking on my dick and swallowing my load of seamen. I, of course, had done the same for him. I wanted to swallow all of him and his seed. We lay like that with our dicks in each other's mouth sucking on dwindling male organs, trying to suck out any remaining fluids. We must have laid dick in mouth for perhaps ten or fifteen minutes. Gert then got up and said for me to wait. He moved around a little and apparently flipped a switch or hit a switch and then I saw them. The shutters over the observation ports started to open and I saw them. I saw the stars. Not twenty or thirty of them; not even hundreds of them; not even thousands of them; but what appeared to be millions upon millions upon millions of tiny bright shining lights that didn't twinkle like they did on Earth. There was no atmosphere or dust to soften the effect. I had not had time on NES or the shuttle ship to look at the stars. Shuttle ships have view ports, but they are mostly for tourists and passengers. Yea, the pilot has a view port that is usually closed for safety reasons. All piloting is done with instruments. Nobody eyeballs anything. First, it is not reliable. Second, you still need your instruments. You rely on them. The big ships have view ports because the scientists and the technicians have to calibrate the ship's instruments so that their observations match the instrument readings. Also the scientists have to be able to directly observe things sometimes.

I sat up and then got up and stood there in awe. Gert said he did the same thing the first time he saw this view. According to Gert, everybody stops or drops whatever they are doing and stares in awe and amazement at the view. You feel like you have died and are speeding your way to heaven. The utter overwhelming majesty of the view is humbling. I do not know if you personally believe in God. I do, but I don't believe that God interferes in our daily lives. He could and he might, but he gave us free will. He has effectively said this is your chance to live your life. Don't fuck it up, please. I don't know what God looks like, but right then and there, I believed that I had per chance gazed upon the face of God himself. The view was that profound. You will have to take my word for it. If you have never seen it in person, it is worth the effort to see the view. Sign up for a trip to the observation port or better yet, the biggest observation port on the ship. Not the one on the moon where the reflected light of the moon obscured even a small part of your vision. Even when the observation port is in dark phase and you look out away from the sun, there is still too much ambient light from the moon's surface and man's activities and that spoils the effect. Imagine a movie screen where the lights are so bright, they each look like tiny suns. Well, they are. The black spaces between stars are so dark and so black, that you can lose yourself in those spaces. Those spaces are so dark and of course, so big, even though they appear small.

Scientists have made time lapse recordings photographically or photonically of even the tiniest spaces of darkness. In each area of darkness the size of an eraser on a pencil, there are not ten, twenty or thirty stars. There are thousands, and tens of thousands of galaxies in each dark space they have examined. There are not solar systems, but galaxies of stars in those empty spaces where the human eye can not detect or perceive any light. Where there is nothing for the eye to see or perceive, there is still stuff. Large empty spaces where nothing exists for the eye to see, and yet there are galaxies too numerous to even count up in the heavens. Those spaces appear to be quite small, but they are not. While all of what I am saying is true, you must come see it for yourself. I had behold the face of God, and Gert had shown it to me. Now I understood his attraction for his work. I had not ever had anything that moved me as much in my life as this experience. I will grant you that first experience with Tobert when we discovered sex and then fucking, was a close second.

I stood up and held Gert to me. We kissed again and swapped a taste of each other. I reached around and rubbed and patted his ass and then finally ran my finger up and down the crack of his ass. I got a little braver and then ran my finger around his hole. He hugged me even closer and then positioned himself so that my finger found his hole and he backed up to my finger and allowed me to enter him slightly with my finger. Yes, here was a man who liked men and knew what he wanted. I reached down and retrieved the lubrication tube and smeared some on me and some on my finger and entered Gert with my finger. I pressed home with my finger and then gradually worked up to two fingers. He opened up without too much trouble. I do not think that he did this too often, but it was obvious to me that he had done it before. Perhaps several times before.

We kissed. I turned him around and we faced up toward the sky with his back toward me. I placed the head of my penis at the entrance to his ass hole. I pressed against his back door and waited for him to open it for me. It only took a few minutes for me to feel Gert working his ass muscles, and I could feel his hole pulsating. Gradually I could feel it opening to let me enter him. Again and again it pulsated, and then Gert opened up enough that when I pressed forward, I entered him. I could feel the head of my dick pop into his ass hole beyond his anal muscle. Gert turned his head and kissed me and said it had been a while since he had let someone enter him and give him pleasure. "Please be gentle with me and don't hurt me. I am not like some woman who is used to this."

"I will go just as slow as you want me to be with you. You are tight, very tight." He was even though he opened up for me. But he was tight. Just because he had had others up there didn't mean he had let everyone up there. I began some slow movements and reached around and felt that Gert had lost some of his hardness. I continued to slowly fuck him and gradually I could feel that he became hard again. "Let me know what angle feels best for you my love."

"It all feels good. I don't usually let anyone enter me, and I would not have, but you are so attractive and such a nice person. I like you very much." He sort of lay back in my arms and I held him up. "I can not climax like this without you or me rubbing me at the same time."

"Well, we can see if we can change that this time. The only condition is that you have to let me know what feels best for you. I want you to thoroughly enjoy this as much as I am, or even more than me."

"How is that possible? I am a man and I know how good it feels to penetrate someone. I know what a man feels when he is penetrating his partner. This pleases me, but it does not feel as good as doing the penetrating."

"Well, then I must show you other ways to do it." With that I withdrew. "Please lie down on your back and face up and look at me, and the stars." With that he laid down on the rug on his back. I lifted his legs and held them up and exposed his ass hole and gently entered him again. I laid his legs up against my chest, one on each side of my head and then hooked his legs over my shoulders. I adjusted myself so that I could fuck him comfortably for both of us. Then I leaned over and kissed him as I made love to his body through his ass hole. I had my arms around the outside of his arms and my body between his legs. We kissed and then I bent over and licked his dick and drew him into my mouth.

"Oh. I love that. That feels so good." He was hooked. I changed the angle at which I thrust myself into him, and I finally found his joy spot. I could feel the little bump inside his ass hole and began to rub and poke that on each stroke. "That's it. Right there. I don't know what you are doing, but that is it. That feels good. Real good. Keep doing that. I love that."

"I have found your secret hidden inner spot. A spot that every man has and many don't know they have. This is called fucking. Do you like it Gert. I am fucking you. Do you like me to fuck you?"

"Yes. Yes, I do. Yes. Yes. Just keep ... You called it fucking me?"

"Yes, that's the old term for it. Do you like it."

"Yes. I love it. Please don't stop. Keep fucking me. Fuck me until I climax."

"That's called cumming. I will fuck you until you cum."

"Yes. Please keep fucking me until I cum if that is possible."

"Oh. It's possible. And I might just keep fucking you after you cum and you will enjoy that even more." I kept this up for perhaps twenty minutes and then I felt Gert's ass hole tighten up more than I thought was possible and then He yelled a little.

"Keep it up. Don't stop. I am almost there. No, you don't have to touch me. Just keep fucking me. Oh. It feels so good." With that I could see another white discharge just drool from Gert's dick from his piss slit. Over and over again I rubbed and bumped his joy spot, then more and more liquid poured forth. Gert kept moaning and groaning. I bent over and licked up his fluid and all of his discharged seed. Finally I bumped and grinned myself into Gert and pumped my seed home filling his ass hole with my liquid essence. I leaned over and kissed Gert. He used his hands to grab my face and hold me to his face as we kissed. I stuck my tongue in and around his mouth and we kissed like long lost lovers who had not seen each other for decades.

Finally we separated our faces, and then gradually we separated our bodies. I lay down on the carpeted area next to Gert. There we lay for a long time just looking up at the stars. They were as beautiful as Gert. When I fell into the spell of the stars, I looked at them with new meaning. Now whenever I see a starry sky, I think of Gert and this time with him. Gert then rolled over, and was all over me and kissed me again. "I have never before experienced this kind of climax when I have been entered before." Gert looked into my eyes with a starry look of a child in love.

"You have never been fucked before?" I asked.

"Yes, I have. A few times. I guess this is the first time anyone has actually made love to me by climaxing inside of me and not just gone there to get his release personally. You actually made love to me. This is the first time that I have felt anything like that happen to me. My whole body shook as you ... fucked... me. It is unlike anything I have ever experienced before. I never knew it could feel that good to be fucked by another man."

"Well, if it didn't feel that good. Why did you let someone fuck you? What ever would be the reason to allow yourself to be fucked if it didn't feel that good?" I couldn't understand why someone would let someone put their dick up your ass hole if it didn't feel good to the person getting fucked.

"Because I liked that person. I wanted to give them pleasure.

I suffered through the pain and the discomfort to give pleasure to the person I wanted to be with. I really liked them and wanted to show them a good time." Gert really was a sensitive, nice and kind person. I am too, but bearing and suffering through that kind of pain with no gain in physical pleasure, is just not something I would do. Gert is a better man than I am. We kissed and ran our hands over each other's bodies, but basically, we were both spent and the evening was over sexually for us. Now was the best time where we could be just share our intimacy of feelings, by talking, touching, kissing and holding each other. Sometimes the best stuff after the passion and urgency of sex has been satisfied. We both had duty in about ten hours and we needed our sleep. I was sure that we would both sleep better this sleep period than we had for weeks.

We got up and kissed and held each other longer. When we could delay the inevitable no longer, we got dressed and went forth ready to face the world. We closed the shutters on the observation port and the world seemed quiet and empty again compared to half the entire universe starting at the two of us having sex under the light of half of the stars of the universe. We held hands and entered the anteroom and closed and secured the hatch to the observation room. We kissed again and then unlocked the door and left together. We talked about the movie and made a date to see another movie in the equivalent of 5 days. That was when they changed the movie showing in the theater. I was looking forward to our next date. I was not sure that anything could top this first date, but I did want time to try and equal this performance in a few days.

Chapter Six

Life on the Galo was settling down to be a routine. I had classes for 4 hours every other day. I rotated among the ship's different specialties to learn the practical aspects of running a ship and worked a four hour shift the second half of the day. On the rest of the days I worked 2, 4 hour shifts and had two days without any shifts. I worked two days and had one off and then three days and had one off. That schedule was changed when we docked when every available man had standby duty to relieve any man injured, too tired to function effectively and to man the automated cargo machines 24 hours a day until we were back in space again. However, because of orbit calculations, we sometimes had 4 or 6 or even 24 hours after cargo had been unloaded and loaded before we shipped out. Then we were granted liberty at a port based on seniority and who had not had liberty recently. The captain and the sergeant tried to be fair to everyone. Everyone, except disciplinary cases got liberty. It is just that some were entitled to more liberty times than others.

To be fair too, there were very few disciplinary cases. Everyone who was in space, wanted to be in space. If you didn't want to be here, then they were more than happy to get you assigned or transferred to wherever you wanted to go. Not to get rid of you, but because they really wanted everyone to be happy about the jobs and duties they were performing. We had such a large complement of medical people because about half of them watched the crew and the other half watched the watchers. They studied interactive personal dynamics. I don't know what that really means, but they made sure that each of us got along with the rest of us. We did carry passengers and emigrants to colonies so a good deal of the time of the psychologists' time was spent in actual interviews supplementing the testing and studies done on earth. The shrinks as we called any of the doctors of the head, spent most of their time sorting out the people immigrating to colonies who would be potential trouble.

No colony needs a trouble maker, malcontent or unhappy person. If you didn't want to be there, they were more than happy to get you out of there. The shrinks also studied how people solve problems. Person problems, social problems and other problems that people have. Problems arising because there are not enough people in the colonies. Problems because there is too much freedom, not enough freedom. They were learning a lot about us as individuals and a collective society by studying the colonies, spaceships of people and learning what makes people tick. And what makes others to tick and then blow up.

The few disciplinary problems we did have were more people who were unhappy because of problems at home. For those people we wanted to get them help. Send them home to get things right with the wife. Get them transferred. Whatever it took. Most people when they get to space, go of their own free will and are quite satisfied being here. We didn't fight wars, and we didn't have constant physical exertions. We just worked. We worked hard and played hard, but not violently. To be fair too, the hard work was not usually physically hard. We had machines to do the hard physical labor. We did the harder work of doing the thinking and keeping ourselves in top physical shape. Sure there was some good natured playing around and jokes, but you didn't joke much around machines and situations that could kill you or your buddy or cause your ship to lose pressure. Those kind of people got weeded out pretty quickly. And believe me, both you, your buddies, and your superiors kept a close eye out for anyone who was unhappy, depressed or not functioning up to optimum. You wanted them to find the problems before they became a problem, and most people cooperated fully. Heck, even I wanted them to find out fast if something was wrong with me before I hurt myself or someone else.

We had psychologists who talked to people and could be seen chatting to everyone. They also had undercover shrink men and women who observed everyone. But nobody resented these people. They were put there to help us. No body was ever told they were crazy and no one ever downgraded anyone. We helped each other, not the other way around. We had one guy whose wife left him and he was shipped home to try and get his family life back together with the understanding that he could come back if and when he wanted. He returned to another ship a year later and had a new wife and a new life. He was assigned to a new ship to start a new phase of his life.

There are some people who never get over some psychological problems. One guy I heard about broke up with his male husband and moped around for a lunar or two. Then one day they found him in an air lock in which the air had escaped. They ruled it an accidental death and his children from his first marriage who were underage got assistance until they were of age and settled into a job or profession. Some people just can't cope with life and living. To them death is a happy ending. I felt sorry for them. Life is too interesting to just walk out on it. But situations like these while few and far between did occur. With the help of the specialists, they were detected and corrected before someone had to clean another airlock.

I was looking forward to my next date with Gert when another bunkmate of mine caught my eye. His name was Joel. He was just 18 and the cutest and most hairy thing I have ever seen. He stood only about 1 ½ meters tall, but he was built like a proverbial brick shit house. He had arms that were the size of my legs and he was constantly working out in the G gym. I don't know how he managed to bulk up out in space. Now don't get me wrong, he was not muscle bound or anything, but while he had the slinder figure of a spaceman, he was on the bulkier side of slender.

Joel had hair growing out of his hairs everywhere. It was thick, dark and slightly curly hair that grew on his chest, on his legs, on his arms and on most parts of his body that I could see. I think that that poor boy had to shave three times a day to be clean shaven. This would not normally interest me, but he was just so cute, so delicious looking and had the tightest, hardest packed looking pair of male buns that he mesmerized me when I saw him naked in the G gym. I virtually drooled over his body. And the problem is that I think he noticed me noticing him. Well, this was not a problem perhaps. He seemed to notice me after I got caught looking at him. Sure we were bunk mates, but so were about 2 dozen other people.

Gert had had to cancel our second date as his duty roster had gotten changed and we made plans to get together in three more days. I think that Joel overheard Gert canceling plans for us to see a movie together so he said he was free and would I like to go. I said sure. I didn't think of it as a date and would just enjoy his company. We had a good time laughing and joking at the movie and talking afterwards. Joel was in communications and he offered to show me the communications room. I figured sure, why not. He brought me to a compartment near the center of the ship and said that he worked in this room and most of the time it was just a 4 hour duty assignment and then the communications for the ship was switched over to another room in another part of the ship. Actually, they had about 10 communications rooms around the ship. They used a different one every 4 hours and that required six rooms per day of 24 hours. The idea was that there was redundancy in the ship everywhere so that if a meteor struck the ship it would not take out all communications. This also gave each communications officer his own domain and his own office. When not in use, the office was not occupied unless needed. Joel had this one for his exclusive use when not being used for training.

I know that this redundancy of ship design was for a safety purpose and it does not hurt to lug around extra communications equipment because everything we did depended on communications, but the office was actually small. It was just big enough for three people to work barely comfortably. However, they did not work with any luxury space. Empty space is not expensive to transport. Mass (weight in Earth terms) costs big bucks to move around space. So the communications room was possibly about 3x3 meters with all the equipment built in and which could be easily removed for quick access. Everything was rack mounted so it slid out and was modular. There was a pull down sleeping platform for one man in the event of an emergency where the radio room had to be manned continuously.

Joel had added his own touch by bringing on his own floor covering and fastening it to the deck with Elephant fasteners. You know, they are the things that hold it down just as if an elephant was standing on it. Elphs (pronounced elfs, for short) were just about the de facto standard fastener used on ships by the laymen and even officers in the space corps. They just worked well and didn't depend on an atmosphere, gravity, or anything. All the normal Earth stuff dried out in a vacuum or the cold of space.

When he shut the door to the communications room and I noticed he locked it, he turned to me and we started talking. "I had a good time tonight. I didn't know you were such fun just to be around when you are not working. You seem a little formal sometimes." He said to me.

"I do try to be efficient, but I didn't think that I was unfriendly." I didn't want to seem stuck up. Nobody here knew of my family's money and I didn't have to live up to or down any expectations. I could just be myself.

"Nobody thinks you're stuck up or anything, but we just don't know how friendly you might want to be as a person." He looked into my eyes. "We know that you are on the fast track to be an officer. Graduating from the Space Academy and doing a tour of duty for a few years. Then you will probably go back for further specialization. Then you will be in line to become a captain or something ten or more years down the line, depending on your aptitude." He looked serious. "We just weren't sure if you were also a regular Joe who we could have fun with."

"Well, that depends. Just what kind of fun did you have in mind?"

"He looked up at me. He grabbed my head and brought it to his and our lips met. I couldn't believe it; he was a good kisser. He had a long tongue and he took command of my mouth and in return took control of me. He made love to my face and when he took control he liked to dominate the person he was with. I do not know if it was because of his short stature, or in spite of it, but Joel was a sexual force to be reckoned with in this ship. I had seen his buns and knew I wanted to get my face between them and get to his little hole, but had to play this carefully. I know that he wanted me and my buns because he immediately started rubbing them and feeling me up. This was good because it gave me the opportunity to feel him up... and down... and everywhere. And I did precisely that. What surprised me was when I learned that he was wearing two jock straps.

We quickly got each other's clothes off and I saw the two jock straps and he admitted that he wore them because of me. "I don't understand that."

"You do this to me baby." With that he pulled them both down and his dick unfolded from beneath the two thick layers of pouch. There I saw not the plaything of a little boy or even a man of 18 years, but the fuck tool of a bull. He must have been at least 22 to 24 cm in length. That was even longer than me and I was big. He was also big around and was just a little bigger around than I was. I was glad that he did not belong to that religion that cut off the skin at the end of a man's dick. Thank goodness. However, I suspected that goodness had nothing to do with it if it was in anywise associated with a dick that big. "I want to transport you to happiness with this."

"I would like to play with it and you. But we need to get one thing understood right here and now. You are not putting that thing inside of me. Not now or ever."

"Oh, baby, you will change your mind when I get half of it inside of you."

"No. I won't. I'll lick it, play with it, suck on it and do lots of things with it, but I would not let you put that thing inside of me unless I am unconscious. And then it would not be consensual. You can't consent if you are unconscious."

"Which ever way you like it?" He had an answer for everything. "Look. Your organ is big too. Almost as big as mine, and I like you. I will let you put yours in me if I can put mine in you. I think we both would like to do each other." He looked a little hurt that if he would let me fuck him that I wouldn't let him fuck me. I believed in equality, but it was not necessary in fucking. I just wasn't meant to be fucked. At least not yet in my young life I thought.

"Well, I will think about it. But not now, and not anytime soon. I just don't think I could take it. And I know that I don't even want to think about taking it. It would hurt and I wouldn't be able to walk for a lunar." I was serious. And he was serious that he wanted to fuck me. I was thinking, maybe in another 15 or 20 years. When I am an old man and looking to settle down for a while and would find a lover I could trust to be gentle and to love me worth giving up my virginity to him. I wanted Joel, but not that way, and not that bad at this time.

We kissed and he went down on my dick and sucked me into his mouth. After a few minutes, he came up for air and I went down on his dick. I couldn't take half of him in my mouth without gagging. We kept this up for some time and then he pulled down the sleeping platform. We lay down naked and hugged each other and fell into a 69 position. Within minutes we each became harder and shot a full load of our seeds into each other's mouths. I could not believe how hairy Joel was. He was like a bear. I loved running my face in his crotch hairs and the hairs on his legs. I loved running my hands over his body and feeling his hair. It tickled my hands and I loved running my lips on the hairs on his balls and all around his private parts. I couldn't understand it, but I loved all his hair. Even his chest was covered in hair and I had to fight to get my lips on his nipples because of all the hair. We kissed and held each other for a long time and then started up sucking on each other again.

This time, we started with a slow suck and even took time off to lick and chew on each other. Then I wandered to his neither region. That is the region between his balls and ass hole. The region that is neither balls nor ass hole. He was hairy, but very clean. Apparently he had to scrub himself clean after he used the toilet each time. This was good, because I wouldn't want to clean it for him. He had a great smell that was of a man. Every man smells different, but they all for some reason, seem to smell sexy. I don't know what there is about a man that is so attractive sexually. But remember, that if you consider a man attractive, what is there not to like. If you don't like the way a clean man smells, then you want something else, because you can't want a man. I am not talking a dirty smelling man, not bathed for three days, but a clean man that still smells like a man.

I stuck my tongue in his hole and cleaned it out for him and he did the same to me, but only after I had apparently overcome his resistance. I reached around and took out my tube of lubrication and applied some to his ass hole and got a finger up inside of him. He was unbelievably tight. I think that he might have been a virgin, if that was possible. Perhaps he only offered to swap fucks with me because he had no intention of returning the favor. He just wanted to get his dick inside of me. I am a cad and I know another cad when I see him, kiss him, or if he wants to fuck me. But I gave him the benefit of the doubt. Maybe he would have returned the favor. I hunted around inside of his ass hole and found that little, firm oval structure and began to gently rub and stroke it. He stopped sucking on my ass hole momentarily. I knew I had found the spot, and that he liked it.

I continued to rub my finger over his hot spot and he gradually took his mouth off my dick and balls and stared outward and was concentrating on something or nothing in particular. I could tell that something was preoccupying his thoughts. I could also feel his body bend and contort to my ministrations of his body. I thought that he was in my power. How well I knew the reactions to someone who was enjoying themselves sexually. Gradually I pressed another finger to his puckered opening and let the excess lubrication smear on that finger. Within minutes I had worked the second finger just inside the opening of his hole. Then it was just a matter of minutes before I had two fingers inside his hole and was rubbing his hot spot with them. Stretching his hole and working his bottom with both fingers. His back was arched and I could feel his hole tightening up and loosening up periodically. He laid his head down and moaned in obvious pleasure and ecstasy.

I thought that I had him now. He was mine for the taking if I just didn't move too fast. I leaned over and took his penis into my mouth and sucked on the head and ran my tongue around the head and tickled under the head at that certain spot that every man knows is very sensitive. Right there just under the head of his dick. The spot where the foreskin comes together at the underside of the head of his dick. A few little licks of the tip of my tongue was all it took for him to cry out softly.

"Oh. Don't stop. That feels so good. Where did you learn this?" I knew I could fuck him now. I also knew that if he couldn't do this to my body, he wasn't getting any where near my ass hole with that weapon of his; especially if he didn't know how to properly use his equipment. He had more than enough equipment, but did he know the proper use to give sexual fulfillment to his male partner. For those men, they might as well be fucking a woman. A woman's hot spot is located just inside of her body and some require their clitoris to be stimulated. Fucking a woman does not require any special knowledge of a man's anatomy. Just a big dick rubbing the woman's clitoris that is located just above her female entrance hole. Ram it in, move it around and back and forth and bingo, you hit even it she doesn't. Then you roll over and go to sleep on her. All activities that are very fulfilling for the man, a big disappointment for the woman. No wonder so many women hate so many men. If that is all men did for me physically; I would hate them too. I certainly wouldn't let them fuck me. Stock answer, you want to put your what in my what? I don't think so. I'll tell you where you can put it. And if it feels so good to you, then you can tell me how you like it.

I kept up my double digital lovemaking and then used my hand to lubricate my dick. I then rolled Joel on to his back and knelt between his legs and sucked on his dick again. Next I positioned his legs over my shoulders and pressed my dick against his tiny puckered hole. I then looked into his eyes and leaned over and kissed him again. I forced my tongue into his mouth and pressed my tool against his hole, and gradually entered him. I traveled up inside of him with back and forth strokes of about four centimeters each. However, I made sure that I went in four cm and pulled back about two cm. Four cm in and back two cm. I then pulled all the way out and ran my lubricated hand over the head of my dick and entered him again. I traveled up his shit highway much easier this time with renewed lubrication. Within minutes I was fully and firmly seated in his hole and moved my dick around until I found his secret hot spot again. I moved the head of my dick around to keep rubbing and bumping his spot.

Back and forth and over and over again, I pushed and prodded his insides. He was again enjoying the feeling. I kept this motion up for the longest time. I leaned over and sucked on his massive tool. I rubbed my tongue around his piss slit in the head of his penis and sucked on his dick. Over and over again and as he approached a climax I stopped and then leaned over and kissed him on his lips, my tongue taking charge of his mouth and letting him taste his juices I was sucking up into my mouth. My mouth was full of his leaking slime that tasted so good to me. I wanted him to share in my flavor of him.

As I fucked back and forth into and drew back out of him, his ass hole would expand on my inward thrusts and contract around me on my backward pull out movements in an effort to keep me inside of him. Over and over again and with each bump upon entering, his dick jerked a little and another drop or two of clear liquid oozed from the piss slit of his penis. We kept up this pure raw animal rutting behavior for perhaps almost a half an hour standard time at which time he made the loudest moans to date. Suddenly I could feel his ass hole tighten up and I saw his dick twitch. Then some white male seed flowed forth from his penis and formed a puddle on his stomach. I leaned over and licked it up into my mouth, but made sure I did not swallow it. I held his seed in my mouth and leaned over and forced my tongue into his mouth. I opened my mouth and let his seamen flow from my mouth to his. He eagerly sucked his seed from my mouth and tongue. I could tell he wanted more.

I had made sure that I had not cum, and kept on fucking him. I put off my climax as long as I could and finally he spoke. "I can't take any more. Please cum and finish your business. You win. You are the better man even though you are not the bigger man. I need you to finish." He was exhausted, but I was not going to stop until he had climaxed again.

"You are not getting off that easy. You tried to insinuate that I didn't know how to fuck a man and give him pleasure. Now you are going to be forced into experiencing more pleasure than you have a right to experience in one fuck. Let alone one night." With that I continued to fuck hard and fast. I centered my attack on that hard spot or nodule inside of his ass hole. Instead of rubbing and stroking it gently, I went out of my way to be sure I bumped and poked it on each inward thrust. Over and over again and again and again he moaned and then his entire body stiffened up and he came and I bent over and sucked his dick so that his seed shot into my mouth another time. Finally I slammed myself into his hole over and over again and deposited my seed inside of him. I had claimed my prize, and I had marked him as mine. He was now mine, any time I wanted him. I controlled his pleasure through his ass hole. From now on, he was mine.

I held him in my arms and we kissed, and I stayed deep inside of him as my dick gradually resumed its normal size. I held his head and moved it where I wanted it and at any angle that pleased me and he willingly complied. I bathed his ears with my tongue and chewed on his neck and sucked his tits. Yes, I was going to enjoy life on the Galo, even if I never met anyone besides my two bunkmates Gert and Joel. Finally we untangled our intertwined bodies and lay down next to each other. We kissed and held each other.

"I never knew that having another man penetrate you could feel so good."

"Of course not." I replied. "Nobody has ever properly fucked you before. That is why I wasn't going to let you fuck me if you didn't know how to do it right." I was still catching my breath. "There is more to fucking than just sticking your penis in a hole and fucking until you shoot your seed. Lots more."

"I am beginning to see that."

"No. Now you know that there is. And maybe next time when I fuck you again, you will learn some new techniques." We kissed some more and had tender exchanges of affection with our hands and tongues and lips all over each other's body until we had to get up and get dressed. It was getting late. We kissed again and then exited the communications room and walked down the passageway discussing the movie like two shipboard friends.

Chapter Seven

Two days had passed since my date with Joel. Life was good and I was getting into ship board routine. I was now an old hand at this and enjoyed my duty station and the classes. I enjoyed the free time I had and then we had the unloading stop at Ganymede. I know that our last stop at the moon would naturally seem that our next stop would be Mars. But right now, Mars was on the other side of the Sun from us. Well, not the other side, but almost. We would make another run to Ganymede before our next run to Mars. Sure, with hyper drive, we could travel that far in not too much time, but hyper drive is in a straight line and right now that would bring us too close to the Sun for comfort. We do not travel closer than the orbit of Mercury and prefer to stay at least as far away from the Sun as the orbit of Venus. If possible, we would not go any closer than the orbit of the Earth for safety reasons.

For the last 300 years, we have had orbiting satellites around the Sun measuring the solar winds and radiation from the sun in multiple orbital planes and could alert us as early as physically possible of radiation and dangerous conditions. However, when some phenomena travel at the speed of light and all reports travel at the speed of light, then the report of anything out of the ordinary travels as fast as the trouble travels. The only time you get a break is when the phenomena travels at less than the speed of light, and then your warning may only be seconds or minutes. That is why every space hand is trained to respond without thinking to the different warning sounds in a ship.

For meteor showers, the crew goes to the inner compartments of the ship and secures all blast doors. For solar winds, depending on the type, you can go to the inner recesses of the ship behind lead enclosures. For gamma ray bursts, you pray to whatever God you believe in and hope for the best. Even a magnetic field the size and power of the Earth can not protect you and you just hope that it doesn't hit your ship with any force or it hits in a burst that has spread out big enough to cover the entire ship. There was what they later figured out was a gamma ray burst in 2363, that sprayed the Galielo 5. They never recovered it for ten years as she went off in a direction that was the result of being struck in the middle of a course correction maneuver.

About ten years later, they finally caught up with her and when they boarded her everyone was dead. Not just dead, but preserved dead. Apparently it was a strong enough burst to kill all life, even microscopic life and the ship's ventilation systems kept on automatic and the bodies dried out and were just about mummified. Once someone boarded, we brought our germs with us and procedures had to be initiated to preserve the remains of the crew for shipment back home and proper burial. I know in old time sea novels, that they buried people at sea by committing their bodies to the ocean. There they would decompose and be recycled. In the old space novels of the day, they would bury people in space by wrapping their bodies in some canvas and chucking them into space. How barbaric a custom and practice.

Today, we just place the body in cold storage and then deliver it to the next of kin on the designated home planet. We do not routinely just put someone out an airlock and clutter up space with their remains. After a while, that would make the Earth to Moon and space station runs very hazardous to your health. The last thing I want to be is a piece of space garbage that kills someone else because they didn't keep up with my irregular orbit. If a person wants to be buried in space, we do so in an orbit that will send them into the Sun. After all, we now know that every element except hydrogen was created in a sun somewhere. The calcium in our teeth and bones was created in a sun somewhere. Same for all the other elements.

For those who want a proper burial, we can arrange for their body to be reprocessed in our greenhouse, the one that grows flowers and is tended entirely by volunteers under the supervision of a senior horticulturist. There we grow flowers for the ship and a person's atoms are reprocessed into flowers and beautiful things. Their bones are later reclaimed and delivered to the next of kin after decomposition is complete. It is a nice thought. You go on living as living flowers in the ship forever and your bones go home to rest for all eternity. Each man is expected to do volunteer duty in the flower greenhouse. It is considered an honor and a duty to your shipmates to care for their remains. Most of the ship choose this type of services. I had wondered why a working ship that didn't carry many passengers had so many cut flowers everywhere in the ship and mostly in the crew's quarters and duty stations. It was our way of being close to our comrades. Most of who died of natural causes. Our accident rate was very low. I learned that the flowers grown for the passengers were reprocessed in our flower gardens, but none of our comrades were grown for the passengers. They belonged to us. Sort of a duty and an honor that we reserved to our selves alone. I can't explain it, but do a few turns of duty to your comrades and learn of the reverence even the most hardened space traveler has for this duty assignment and you will begin to understand. Here we were all equals caring for each other.

Ship board life and routine suited me well. I saw Gert and Joel every day and couldn't decide whom I liked the best. They were each different and had their own strong and weak points. Neither Joel nor Gert said anything in front of the other nor in front of any other men. But when we were alone, each put the moves on me to get together again. And the worst part was, I wanted to get together with each of them again. Several times again, but trying to find the time was getting hard to do. Docking with the shuttle at Ganymede was fun. We unloaded cargo, machinery and other required supplies that could not be manufactured on Ganymede and were usually bought by the colony collectively. We were able to pick up certain manufactured items, usually requiring a lot of individual labor such as knitted sweaters, and items that could not be made conveniently on Mars or the Moon. We transported them to those places and made a profit on the freight. They just didn't find it profitable to raise sheep on Mars, but Ganymede was being terra formed and the animals adapted to the lower gravity and lower atmospheric pressure of Ganymede better than most people.

Thus there was sufficient extra wool to export. Made into sweaters and other items, they sold well on the Moon and Mars. There were lots of exports like that. Lots of cheeses, dairy and meat products that were in high demand everywhere but Earth. With population control on Earth, there were no more food shortages. It was just more expensive to lift it on the beanstalk than to transport it from Ganymede. However manufactured items were in short supply everywhere off world and Earth produced them in abundance.

Mars was being terra formed, but it was a much more difficult task. First, Mars did not have a liquid iron center or core and did not have a magnetosphere which we believe resulted from the movement of the liquid iron core. This is long and involved, but that magnetosphere kept the solar winds away and helped to retain an atmosphere. See basic planetology 101 at the Space Academy. There is more to it than just that, but that's the basic principle. Secondly, Mars was bigger and it would take longer to terra form her. Lastly, Mars didn't have the water in as much supply as did Ganymede. Until they struck water in greater abundance in Mars, notice I said in and not on Mars, the most common export to Mars would be water and manufactured items.

On Ganymede men lived on the surface because of the terra forming, but men still lived under the surface of Mars, inside Mars in the tunnels. They had miles of pressurized tunnels under the surface of Mars and at least a dozen giant tunnel boring machines operating at any one time creating more tunnels. Most of the tunnels were between 500 and 1,000 meters below the surface to allow for sufficient solid stone between a pressurized tunnel and the surface. There were surface tunnels, that is tunnels to the surface frequently, but they all had air locks on them and they were for safety purposes and to be able to access the surface to feed the solar power to the tunnels and the like. There were several levels of tunnels, but any large tunnel usually didn't have much above or below it for safety reasons. The multilevel tunnels were from the old original tunnel structures and many of them were almost large caverns. Actually, more like one tunnel that had been subdivided and appeared to be two or three tunnels.

The engineers had their test results and knew how much stress the rock could take and where it was the weakest and where we could put new tunnels. The maps of the different Mars cities were all kept on computer because it would have taken four or five planes of displays to represent each city. Remember, when you are off world, you can't assume that any section of a city or a planet is flat like it is on Earth. There is just too much good space in ample abundance on Earth to worry about building twelve different street levels in a city. You can go up, but that is in a building and buildings have street addresses. It is almost like having one large building the size of Manhattan Island with as many as 5 or 6 floors and all interconnected in the most screwed up connections you can imagine. Not screwed up on purpose, but built according the stresses that the rock can support with safety in mind. I know; I tried studying it on the computer maps. I gave up and when I am in Mars, I just rent a portable gyroscopic inertia locator (Gil.) On Mars, I don't go anywhere without a Gil. But I am getting ahead of my story.

We were off loading machinery and mechanical supplies for Ganymede. We had some food items, that were more difficult to produce easily on Ganymede. We did import some petrochemical products for plastics synthesis. No fuels, because they used either atomic piles to generate power or solar cells. The cells were not that efficient, that far from the Sun, but there was plenty of land and solar cells were passive and produced energy on land that was not cultivated. There was not enough of a thick atmosphere like on Earth to make wind any source. Nor was there any running water to waste letting it run down hill to generate electricity.

We did ship a lot of Earth's CO2 to Ganymede. This was good for Earth to get rid of it and Ganymede separated the carbon and released the oxygen. Ganymede was able to cleave the carbon through either photo synthesis or chemical reactions using catalysts. Earth needed to get rid of the carbon dioxide and right now Ganymede needed it. A mutually beneficial relationship for both worlds. Of course, the little bit we could export from Earth didn't make much of a dent in our levels, but since the almost total ban of carbon dioxide producing reactions on Earth and close monitoring of all CO2 producing processes, the balance is being restored to stabilize the climate of the Earth. Hopefully this is before we manage to kill ourselves off by modifying the climate so much that the ecosystem is irreparably damaged.

We also carry lots of dehydrated water off world. That's a space corps joke. You know. Dehydrated water, you just add water to it. Well, never mind. We do transport some water when space and weight are available. They ship clean clear water any time the beanstalk is not busy lifting more precious cargo. We have enough to spare on Earth to supply the known world with enough water to recycle it and keep people alive. Not enough to fill an ocean or anything. We couldn't transport that much, but tens of thousands of liters each trip we can and do transport for off world use. Sometimes even more water is shipped to put reserves on each of our colonies on every world. Reserves of that most precious thing, water, after air to breathe. Sure they recycle it off world just like we do on Earth. However, our little additions to the balance sheet were significant. Mother Earth does it for us at home automatically.

Off world we have had to create the complete recycling systems ourselves. It is not hard to do, but we have to be certain that we can properly filter or distill out the water and leave behind the human sludge and all other wastes. That was something we started learning even before we colonized the moon. We had to get the basic principles down just for the first rudimentary space station that circled the earth. But don't think that just because we leave behind the waste and sludge from the water, we don't throw away the sludge or put it in land fills. Well actually we do put it in landfills, but we use it to make good dirt after we crush up the rocks and grind them up and make them into a powdery dirt. We add that worthless sludge and then add back in the proper soil bacteria and you can make good rich farm soil out of sterile crushed rock dust. There is nothing like good old manure, human or animal, for a natural fertilizer. We don't have to import it, and it works just great.

This was just some of the basic things I learned at the Space Academy. However, learning about it and actually tending to the systems in space where your life and the lives of your friends depended upon it is different. It has to be working perfectly and without a hitch. That is completely different. Believe me, it is just different when your own life depends on your job being performed exactly correct. On Ganymede we just loaded the shuttles that carried the containers to the surface, and containers were ready to be transported back to fill our cargo holds with their exports. Dull and boring except that when we had liberty, we were allowed to go to the surface. I went, it was interesting, but the prices for everything were high. Native produced things were cheap such as the things I mentioned. But I didn't need anything made of wool. The meat produced there was great and a steak was cooked and looked like half a cow for only 5 standard dollars. One fifth the price it would be on Mars and three times the size. The girls, which many a space corps member chased looked only passable. Frontier life is hard on the women. However, the men looked good, but I didn't want to get caught with a local. They might want to roll a spaceman for money or fun. You don't want to take a chance you'll miss your shuttle back.

However, on Ganymede you didn't see too many M-M couples. Most people who migrate off world want a place to raise a family with lots of kids and lots of room. Why would anyone work so hard to build a new life if you don't have kids to pass it on to. On Earth you had to have permission to have a child and for a woman to have her fertility turned on. On Ganymede you could have as many children as you wanted. Children in a farming community meant good workers. It was cheeper to grow the people and animals they needed on Ganymede than to ship them up from earth. Tractors broke and had to be repaired and used fuel. Nobody ever put two tractors together and got another tractor. On the other hand, you put a male and a female horse together and you got more horses. This was simple basic common sense and basic biology. So there were lots of large families which normally would be unheard of on earth. There were some M-M people, I imagine, and couples, but Ganymede was still a rural agricultural colony. I understood that many of the M-M people or couples went to Earth. Under the repatriation Act of 2276, all people who could trace their ancestry back to Earth, (let's be realistic that's where we all came from) could go back to Earth and be a citizen it they wanted. They had to pay their own way, but Earth would take you. Regardless of population control, you could come to Earth. It is no use trying to maintain a colony or civilization with unhappy people. Most people on a colony were sacrificing today for a better tomorrow. Some were just pioneer types who didn't mind the hardships. You might think that some were criminals and malcontents that had to ship out to the colonies. Not in today's day and age, Earth had too much invested in the colonies. To get each person to a colony, train them to feed themselves required lots of effort. They didn't send criminals or anyone who didn't want to go. It was hard to be selected for a free trip unless you had a desired skill. Incorrigible criminals were just sent to one of several islands in the pacific or some other ocean. If you did something bad enough to be committed there, then you deserved what you got. There we are talking deliberate murder, people who are just violent and dangerous to be around in a civilized society.

If I were to declare myself a M-M, my biggest problem is my family being disappointed. Nobody beats up on M-M's any more. That has not happened for centuries. I read about it in some of the old history books. If you are an M-M, your family can not disinherit you.

You are entitled to your birth right. But they don't have to give me discretionary funds or associate with me. Probably most of my friends would still be my friend, but some would shun me as a choice. Of course if they don't like the girl I marry, they can shun me too. So you make your choices in life and you move on. You can't please all the people all the time. You have to please yourself or you are nothing but a social prostitute. You are selling out who you are for acceptance as someone who you are not.

However, while on Ganymede, I did see some fine ass specimens of manhood. Apparently, someone noticed that I noticed them. I was sitting in the bar and when I went to the rest room, this fine ass young man followed me in. As in all civilized societies, all rest rooms service all sexes. Once there, you entered a private room to actually take care of business. As I entered the anteroom, this little stud followed me and then he quickly opened the door to a private room. He looked at me and held the door open. He looked at me again and then motioned me with his head to follow him in. Like a fool, I did. I was scared to death, but he was so fine looking, and I was horny. It was at least four days since my last sexual encounter. Once inside he locked the door and he turned toward me and ran his hands over my body. He was not more than about 16 years old, but was of the age of consent even here. They had many women with a child at his age. He was tall, almost as tall as I was, but he still had the body of a young man about to reach his peak of perfection.

He reached underneath of my shirt and ran his hands over my bare chest and gave me chills of anticipation. I removed my shirt and helped him with his shirt. He reached his hands into my pants and tried to rub me and get to my dick. He couldn't because my pants were too tight. He then ran his hands on the out side of my parents and felt how hard I was and I did the same to him. We both wanted this real bad.

"Have you ever been with anyone?" I questioned.

"No. Not yet. There are not many of us here and not many in this city. I want to try to be with a man and I figured that coming to this bar would be the best place to pick up a space man. Someone who may not be an M-M, but wants to have sex because his wife or girlfriend is back home and he doesn't know anyone here on Ganymede."

"Well, you are partially right. I don't know anyone here, and I do like your looks. I do want to have sex and I would like to have it with you." I looked around looking a little worried. "How long do we have in here before someone will come looking for us or you?" I was getting not a little but a lot worried.

"Don't concern yourself. There is no charge for these rooms; any charg   e is included in the price of the drinks. Alcohol is cheap here it being a byproduct of the atmosphere project at the tera form stations. Nobody will bother us here for hours if we want to stay here that long. These rooms are frequently used for meetings. That is why I bought a drink and tipped the bartender. We will be fine."

"You come here often?"

"No, but money is the universal lubricant, it makes all wheels turn. I asked the bartender if I could bring a girl back here." He was resourceful, if nothing else. And he was awfully cute. "He said okay and I tipped him." He reached over and loosened my pants and started removing them. I could see his breathing becoming heavy. Soon I was standing naked before him. I was hard and he ran his hands over my body and my hardness. I bent over and unfastened his pants and helped him remove them. He was a big little man and even though he was only about 15 cm in length, it was a very nice pert little tool that stood at attention for me. He looked at me sheepishly.

"I know I am not very big, but I sure am interested in you."

"Size is not the most important thing. I think that you are beautiful. I just love being with a real person who is interested in being with me." I reached up and brought his head toward mine and brought his face to mine. I touched my lips against his and he hesitated. Then I pushed my tongue into his mouth and he surrendered to me. I held his body against mine and I could feel his clear fluid oozing onto my body from his tool. We kissed and he was limp in my arms. Then he sunk down to his knees, and he licked my hardness. He put the head of my dick into his mouth. "That feels so good. Keep it up and you soon will get your reward." It did not take long and soon I filled his mouth with my discharge.

He stood up and we kissed again. Then to his amazement, I bent down and took him into my mouth and returned the favor for him. Within minutes I could feel him tighten up and then he gave his copious discharge to me with loving care and then slumped over my head and back. I kept up my oral ministrations upon him and he became too sensitive. He quickly withdrew himself from my mouth despite my intention to hold him as long as he wanted.

"You have to let go. It is just too sensitive. I can't even stand to be touched by myself; let alone somebody else after I have my climax."

"I just want to please you and give you sexual satisfaction."

"Oh you have. I never thought anyone would want to take my penis into their mouth and cause me to discharge into their mouth. And then to swallow it."

"What's wrong with that?"

"Nothing, but I thought that I would have to do the space corps members and they wouldn't want to do it to me. Why would they? Once they get their pleasure, why would they care about me and more important, why would they put me inside of their mouth?"

"Because they are enjoying doing you as much as you enjoy doing them."

"But you're not an M-M, are you?"

"No, I am not registered nor do I show any symbol, but I enjoy doing this stuff too or why would I have followed you in here?"

"I didn't know, but I was hoping. I never hoped for... this much cooperation from you."

"Why not?"

"I just don't know any other M-M's here and I have never been off Ganymede to know anything else. They don't write books about finding men to have sex with that I know of or can get my hands on."

"Well, how did you figure out how to get me."

"I didn't figure it out, I just wanted you so desperately that I was willing to go and proposition you if I needed to, to get your attention."

"You have a very pretty little ass and cute smile and beautiful eyes. I had made up my mind that if you were available, if there was any way possible, I was going to get to know you." I stopped for a moment. "I have seen at least one here because he wore the symbol."

"I am sure there are more than just Calvin who wears that thing as if it were a badge of courage. I am sure of it, but I don't know how to find them and certainly don't know if they go anywhere to meet or what they do."

"I can't help you there. But if you declare yourself, then you can try and find someone for you. There is such a collection of male flesh around here that surely someone else must want you."

"I think they do, but they only want me to do them and they don't care about my happiness. They would use me and then tell all their friends and they would all come to me to help them out of their problem. I would have all the friends I want, but no one who cared about me or my happiness."

"Now you know how some women feel."

"No. I don't. Because as a woman, I could get a man to marry me and support our children if I wanted to. I could use sex to get him."

"You only think that. But any woman who uses sex as a tool to get a man has a hard time keeping him after she gives it up or after the marriage. Sex should be because of love, not blackmail." All this time I was rubbing his body and getting him ready for the next round. I kissed him again and started rubbing his back side. I ran my finger in the crack of his ass and rubbed his hole.

"Why are you doing that?"

"Because I like you and want to show you even more pleasure."

"Yea. Right. And how. And if it is what I am thinking, then the answer is no."

"What are you thinking?"

"That you want to play with my elimination hole."

"I already am playing with your hole. The question is does it feel good?"

"Yes, but you are not doing anything with it."

"I know, but I can with your permission."

"Why would I give you permission?"

"Because it feels good, and I can make it feel even better." I wanted him to want me. "Do you trust me."

"I don't even know you. I don't know your name and why should I trust you?"

"No reason. But you can. I don't want to hurt you and I want you to feel good. I sincerely do want you to feel good." I hesitated for a few seconds. "I want you to feel good and I can prove it to you."

"How?"

"Let me show you." With that I kissed him and rubbed his hole and then played with it and gently inserted just the tip of my finger into his hole a little." I took my every ready tube of lubrication out of my pocket and put some on my finger tip. I then pressed it against his hole again and eased my finger inside of him. He resisted a little, but did not fight me.

"Oh. Ahhh. That feels different."

"I have had lots of different reactions, but never heard that one. Believe me; you are going to love this. It will feel great."

"What are you going to do to me?"

"I am gradually going to put more and more of my finger inside of you and then another finger if you want it. Then you will tell me what to do." I worked my finger back and forth inside of him and then I reached all the way inside and found his bump or lump. I stroked it and he began to melt in my arms.

"That feels good. I like that."

"I do too. And I knew you would like it." I gradually put a second finger inside of him and then moved them both around and tickled his magic spot. Over and over again, I rubbed him and he finally told me not to stop. He liked me doing this to him. "What do you want me to do now?"

"What do you mean?"

"Well, do you want me to continue rubbing you there?"

"Yes. Yes. Don't stop."

"Well, I could do it better if my fingers were longer."

"This is good enough."

"But it would feel better if I had longer fingers."

"Well, you don't. So don't worry."

"Well, I have something that is longer and would feel better."

"Like what."

"Like my dick."

"Your what?"

"My dick. That's my penis."

"You want to put your penis up my elimination hole?" He hesitated. "No. I don't think so."

"Yes. I think so. You will love it."

"No. I won't and it will hurt."

"I can't lie to you. It might hurt at first. But it would soon feel real good and you will be begging me to put it inside of you."

I kept rubbing him and then I stopped. "What do you want me to do?"

"I want you to keep rubbing me. Rub me with your fingers."

"It will feel better with my dick." He hesitated. He didn't say no, and so I took that as consent. I put lubricant on my dick and had him set down on the toilet seat. I raised his legs into the air and prepared to enter him. I leaned over and kissed him. I told him, "I like you. I will try not to hurt you. You will like this I am sure. But please don't tense up. The more tense you are, the harder it will be for both you and me."

"But you are so big and it hurts."

"Kiss me again and pretend like you are taking a shit, you know relieving yourself and eliminating wastes." I felt him relax a little. His hole opened more for me and I slid inside of him.

"Oh, that hurts." I bent over and kissed him again and then I took his dick in my mouth and sucked on him. "Oh that feels good. Keep doing that. Don't stop and maybe I can stand it." I started moving back and forth inside of him and bent him so that the head of my dick struck the inside of him right behind what would be the back side of his dick. With each bump he oozed more fluid into my mouth. I wanted to keep this up for a long time, but knew I was pushing the limits here inside of this public bathroom. Soon he was flowing like a river into my mouth and I sped up and was ready to empty my seed into him. I wanted to be certain that he also had a second climax and I sped up my lip movements on his tool and could tell that he was close. When he was cuming, I slammed into his ass hole and emptied myself inside of him and sucked his seed out of him and let him empty himself in my mouth.

"Does it still hurt?" I had to tease him.

"Yes. A good kind of a hurt. What did you do to me? That felt better than anything I have ever felt before."

"I fucked you."

"You what to me?"

"That's the old Earth slang for having sex with you and putting my penis up your ass hole. It also applies to a woman when you put your penis in her vagina. But if you put your penis, a dick, in someone's elimination hole it is also sometimes called corn holing them."

"We grow corn here so I can imagine how that got its name. The old timers here talk about what they had to use sometimes to wipe themselves when they had no supplies from earth before we made our own paper for use here. I used to think they were kidding me. There are some things you just don't want to run out of."

"How did it feel? You enjoyed it didn't you." I looked him straight in the eye and he smiled.

"Yea. It did. You ...fuck great. It felt great. How did you learn to do that?"

"Just reading books about other guys fucking guys."

"But you seem to be looking for something and making sure I was feeling good. You didn't just stick your ...dick in me and fuck away."

"Well, it is almost that easy. But a guy has a thing inside him and if you find it and rub it and bump it then he feels good too. That's the only reason guys like to get fucked. If done right, the more they get fucked, the more they like it." I hesitated a little and continued. "And if done right, a guy likes to get fucked even after he cums and can cum and cum again and again. Well, he doesn't give me his seed each time, but it feels like he keeps cuming to him."

"What do you mean cuming?"

"That's when a guy has his climax. That's another old Earth slang word for a man having his climax. He cums."

"I noticed that even though I could not bear for you to touch my penis, sorry dick, when you rubbed the inside of my ass hole and it felt good. I liked that." He smiled at me. "When can we do this again." He was an eager pupil and I was a willing teacher.

"Perhaps in a lunar or two. Depending on when my ship returns."

"I don't think I can last that long. I want you every night to ...fuck me and make love to me." He was serious. "I come from a large family and I am the youngest son. Our family has worked and improved lots of land. My parents have told me that I can have enough land and they have a section about 10 km from them that I can have when I want to settle down. Let's see. You still measure things in acres on Earth don't you. It is about 300 acres of land or a little more. I have a small pond on it that I have put in for the livestock. The pond is being stocked with fish. In another three cycles, we can even fish there once the ecosystem is being established. The house is not yet built, but there are two barns there. One barn is for livestock and another for the chickens, and other fowl and small animals. There is a separate pig area. I have planted some trees that will give us some nice woods."

"I am not sure I want to be a farmer." I didn't want to disappoint him and I wasn't going to jump ship. He looked me in the eyes and continued.

"You don't have to be a farmer. You can be a farmer's husband.

Marry me and we can live there and be happy for the rest of our lives. Just suck me and fuck me every night and I will work to support both of us. You can learn to cook if you want, but I will earn the money and support us and provide for us. I just want to be happy in life."

"You are beautiful and gorgeous." I told him. "If you declared your M-M status, I am sure that many nice young men would jump at a chance to get into that tight little hole you have and treat you real good and nice, every night. As often as you want they will treat that hole nice for you. You don't need me."

"You're right. I don't need you. I like you and I want you. I don't need you, but I want you. I don't want just anybody."

"How right you are. You shouldn't settle for me. Just because I happened to come by."

"You didn't happen to come by. I picked you from all the guys in the room. I was attracted to you and when I saw what you had in your pants, I was scared, but I wanted you so bad, that I didn't care about the pain and any hurt."

"But that is no reason to want to marry me. You don't know me. I could be a criminal or worse."

"You know as well as I do that they don't let criminals go out into space."

"Well maybe I am a criminal and my crimes haven't caught up to me yet." He looked up at me and continued.

"I never did this with anyone else. You were my first."

"And didn't you think that whoever you picked might not want to settle down."

"To live on over 300 acres of land that has already been improved. Here that is a small fortune. My brothers and sisters have all worked so that each of us can have a good start in life. Here you can sell off the land and retire for life. But I am a young man and I love the work and enjoy running a farm. I can hire people to work for me and we have the machinery that we share in the family to work the land.

I have helped my older brothers work their land and they have helped me to establish my land so that I can provide for my self in life. Here we are considered wealthy by any standards. I know that money doesn't mean anything to me if I am not happy. I just though a space man who earns a decent wage would be happy to have a nice roof over his head and lots of food on the table and a cute guy to fuck each night."

"Many of them would. But what would you have done if I had been straight and only interested in you for a blow job?" He looked at me funny.

"A what?"

"A blow job. That is when you perform oral sex on a man." I let it sink in. "What would you have done if that is all I wanted."

"That's simple. I would have given you a ....blow job two or three times a day for the rest of your life."

"Even if I never returned the favor or fucked you?"

"Well, all I ever thought there was for a guy to do to another guy was a blow job and I never expected you to do that to me too. Most guys wouldn't want to do that. I didn't know anything about fucking. So I never considered that or thought that I wanted a guy to put his dick up inside of me and to fuck me. I never knew I wanted it."

"Well, you know now."

"And I want it. I want your dick up inside of me every night, all night long."

"Didn't it hurt a little."

"No. It hurt a lot. But I want it and I will let you stick your dick in me anytime you want to. All night long if you want to. You would never have to take it out if you don't want to."

"Well, what if I have to get up in the middle of the night to piss?"

"You don't have to. You can stay inside of me and do it there. I don't ever want you to have to take yourself out of me." He looked up a little sheepishly. "I love you and want you to marry me." He pleaded with me with his eyes. "Will you marry me?"

"Marry you. I like you. I don't even know your first name and you don't know mine."

"What is there to know. Whatever your name is does not matter to me. I fell in love with your body and your personality. If you were such a bad person I could have figured it out by now. You don't know who I am and you don't know that we have some money in land, so you wanted me for me and not anything else."

Wrong. I wanted you for your cute little fuckable ass and tight hole. I didn't care who it was attached to."

"Right, and I picked you because you had three legs and not two. That third leg between your other two legs. That third leg that can keep me satisfied and not complaining. I think your face is funny, your hair is all wrong, your nose is pointed up in the air and your hands are not pretty. I just like that third leg." I think my feelings were hurt, then I asked him.

"Is that true?" For my own self confidence I needed to know.

"Of course not. But I will tell you anything to get you to marry me or at least stay here and fuck me every night." I felt relieved that he didn't think I was ugly and had all those problems. "I told you I was attracted to you when I first saw you."

"You can't help it if you are attracted to guys with funny faces, wrong hair, nose stuck in the air and ugly hands."

"Oh, but they aren't like that at all. Now you think that I don't like you."

"I have to get back to my ship because the shuttle leaves in two standard hours and I have to walk back to the shuttle station."

"We have time for one more fuck."

"Not for me to walk back to the shuttle station."

"No problem. I can drive you back there in about 15 minutes. You can ride with me in my tractor." Maybe he was telling me the truth. Not that many people had tractors unless they had some money. I didn't want any of his money, I had enough of my own, but I wasn't going to tell him. My family could probably have bought 10,000 acres of land on Ganymede. However, that may have exhausted their wealth because improved land is very expensive on Ganymede and anywhere. Unimproved or not proved land, bare rock or land that had not had crops raised on it for several years and seeded with what was called "paydirt" locally, was considerably cheaper.

Paydirt was the enriched soil culture designated for a particular planet or moon. The good old fashioned dirt of Earth is wonderful for growing things. Just about anything, including things that we don't want to grow. Like all sorts of bad germs they don't have here. If you cut yourself here, you didn't have to worry about tetanus, anthrax, rabies and about a hundred other things. They had the antitoxins stored here for emergencies and everyone here got vaccinated before coming off world or once here. We want to keep up mankind's immunity collectively. We never sent the germs off world, only the vaccines. Also everyone got vaccinated on Earth and elsewhere.

Fuck people being given a choice. If a person got sick and disabled because of a vaccine, then they were put on a pension benefit and allowed to earn some money to supplement their income. We had free enterprise. We had a free enterprise system. But once you get rid of the people who run the government getting rich, then government can be run efficiently and for very little money compared to what it used to cost to run the government. I will tell you what they used to do in the old days. I read about that and couldn't believe it, so I will have to tell you and then you won't believe it either. But it really happened. I will get to that too later. First, I wanted to tell you about paydirt. You had to breed paydirt about a quarter of a cubic meter at a time. Each season the soil culture would spread and grow and enrich the soil in a growing pattern out from a core of enriched "live" dirt. The best thing to make good dirt out of was decaying organic matter. Cow and horse droppings, decaying vegetable matter, like garbage, uneaten food stuffs and even human feces assuming your population was healthy. You mix that altogether after you sterilize it, then seed it with paydirt and in a season you have good bacteria and things growing in the entire live dirt. This was like an old fashioned compost heap on Earth. You do this over and over again until the entire land is composed of good proven soil. In the mean time, you can grow grasses to hold the soil physically in place. The root systems are a good prevention to soil erosion. The decaying root system provides pathways for the next crop to send out its roots. It would take years to improve 300 acres. That is why my little friend was rich. However, once his family had a few hundred proven acres, it was a simple matter over ten years to move large soil areas to the new unproven areas to seed them. You could then move back in the sterile soil and mix it with the proven soil. Within one season or two, the unproven soil would be completely assimilated in the old proven soil.

It was a simple matter to take about 3 or 4 cubic meters of good rich dirt and distribute it over about twenty square meters of sterile soil and in one season enrich the new soil. The 3 or 4 cubic meters of unproven soil you remove you return to fill in the hole of the donating place. You then mix that in over twenty or thirty square meters of good soil and next season or two, the land and soil had healed itself. Unless you had lots of land and lots of man hours to burn, it wasn't worth it. He had a large family and family takes care of their own. He was a rich man in more ways that money could not measure. All he wanted out of life was to be happy. How I wish, I could make him happy. He probably worked on his family's farm from sun up to sun down. When the work was done on the family farm, he worked on the farms of his brothers and their families. Of course his parents saw to it that they all helped out each other. At his ripe old age of about 18, he had been taught the value of land and of hard work. I noticed that he had a nice set of muscles. Not overly developed, but what could you expect. He was used to hard work, but how hard was it to lift something on a moon where everything weighed less than one-third of what it weighed on Earth.

All of this discussion went on in my head in a matter of moments as my education flashed back before my mind. I knew education was good for something, but when you are YDFOC (that's young, dumb and full of cum) you don't seem to pay attention to much unless you think it is going to get you laid. We might have time for one more fuck if we hurry and he gives me a ride back to the shuttle station.

"Well, what do you have in mind?" I asked him.

"Fuck me again and this time kiss me the entire time. I don't care if I don't cum, I just want you inside of me and kissing me. Then, if you can, I want to feel you filling me full of your baby seeds." That was music to my ears. I greased him and myself up again and slowly entered him. He tensed up, but allowed me to enter him. He placed his arms around my neck and held me to him and kissed me as if his life depended upon it. I kissed him back and then started to fuck him for the second time. I moved him around until I could feel that little bump inside his ass and I made sure that I struck it as often as I could. I could see the pleasure in his eyes and the tears running his cheeks. I kissed them and tasted the salt upon his face.

"Does that feel good to you."

"You know it does. Can't you tell."

"Yes, but what turns me on is for you to tell me. I love to hear you talk to me during sex. I like to know that I am pleasing you. Every time I push into you I want to know that you want me to do it to you, and that you like the feel of me inside of you."

"Yes. Yes, I do my lover. I love feeling your big fucking dick inside of my ass hole fucking my ass hole. Even just talking about it with the language you taught me turns me on. I like talking about your big dick in my ass hole and feeling how hard it gets while you put you love inside of me. I want you to put all you baby seeds inside of me and to fill me full of your sex and your love. I want you to do it to me over and over again. Every day and every night as often as you want and for as long as you want."

That was all it took to turn me on. I kissed him harder and got ready to get my nut. I reached down with a free hand and manipulated his cute little dick and ran my finger under his foreskin. I could feel his fluid coming from his head. I ran my finger in his slippery substance that was pouring forth from him and rubbed it all over the head of his dick, and then he hit his stride. His body buckled and tensed under me and when his hole closed up on me I hit too. I pumped my seed into him and felt his seed spew forth and land on my hand and on his belly. Finally he broke our kiss and tears were streaming from his eyes. I licked them up and we kissed again. I held my hand up and licked his seed and swallowed it. He pulled my hand down and licked what was left of his essence from my hand. I then took my hand and collected what had spilled on his stomach and he licked that from my hand too.

Slowly I pulled out from him and he sat there while I stood before him. He leaned over and took my dirty dick that had just come out from inside of him and took me into his mouth and sucked me clean. "I would lick every part of you clean every night if you would only come live with me. I would flip you over and clean your hole with my mouth every day if you wanted me to, if only you would marry me and come live with me. I would do everything in the world to make you happy."

"What I did with you, my friend, I did because I like you. I am an honest man and do this for fun and for love. Don't offer me money and make me nothing more than a male whore. We can do it anytime you want, but not for money. I will be coming back to Ganymede on the next run the ship makes. I will save up some accumulated leave and perhaps we can spend a few days together. That's the best I can offer you. I don't want your money and I don't want to be bought or even tempted. I want you just because I like you, not because of what you can offer me."

"But I don't care."

"I know. And that is very flattering and some of what makes you cute and irresistible to me. But I do care. I care about what I think of myself even if you don't."

"How will I get in touch with you?"

I gave him my personal pad code and he gave me his. I looked down and saw that his name was Cyryl. I had to be careful. I was picking up enough boyfriends that sooner or later, I was going to mix up my boyfriends and not get their names right. This could get to be dangerous or at the least, embarrassing. We got dressed and each left a few minutes apart. We made arrangements to meet outside and he would give me a lift to the shuttle station.

I got into his tractor. Actually, it was more of an all weather vehicle. It had plastic panels that snapped in and out to shut out the weather, temperature and dust, and removed to open up for summer. Maybe I should reconsider his offer. Obviously he was well to do in this society. I could retire here at my ripe old age and just be married to him and live happily ever after for the rest of my life. But no, I thought. I wasn't ready to settle down, but he sure was tempting. He dropped me off at the shuttle station with a half hour to spare. I met with the rest of my crew members who were on leave wandering back. We chatted and then got ready to blast off.

Chapter *Eight*

As we chatted in the shuttle station, I thought back upon the lessons at the academy. The pull of gravity was about 1/4 of that of Earth and so it was not near as expensive to lift mass off Ganymede as compared to Earth. Plus, with the modified gravity lifters, the shuttles are capable of canceling a good portion of the effect of Ganymede's gravity so that the cost per pound was negligible in the whole scheme of things.

Let me set the record straight. You can't cancel gravity or even shield yourself from it, but that is what we laymen call it. Actually, you effectively shield a portion of the mass of the ship from the gravitational field of Ganymede or whatever planet or moon you are near. Just like some radiation shielding can protect you from radiation, we can shield some of the effects of gravity. This is also like a diamagnetic substance shields you from the magnetic fields of a magnet. This does not enable you to float up from the surface, but a 10,000 ton weight which would only weigh about 3,000 tons on Ganymede may only require the same energy to lift as would a 1,000 ton object without the induced shielding. I say induced, because the shielding is not a thing that exists, but a condition in space produced with the use of force and energy in a quantum field.

I don't even understand it, but I did study it and this is about all I can tell you without the mathematics to show you. It doesn't exist in reality, it only exists in mathematics and that is where we discovered it. From there, we found practical applications for its use. I guess in theory you could completely cancel the effects of gravity in a given area of space, but that would require almost infinite energy. Nobody has been able to produce it yet. There is some thinking that perhaps that was the source of the energy of the big bang and why everything the in Universe moved out from a central bang center faster than the speed of light, but that's just conjecture on the part of those scientists who believe in that theory. Everything sounds logical to the people who believe in it.

As we took off, I looked back at the surface of Ganymede. On Ganymede there were not too many tall buildings as that cost a lot in time and effort to construct for a growing world. There were a lot of buildings because one and two story buildings could be made out of the slabs of stone that you could cut from the rock. Like building the pyramids on Earth. Only much smaller structures and square and rectangular ones with roofs made of metal or plastics and doors that were pressurized. Since there was no weather to speak of to wear down the rock and ground, once the surface was formed, unless there was a fault or such, the ground could support any structure you wanted. There was no dirt unless we made it dirt by crushing the rock. Everything was rock. You leveled the ground and placed your building on the ground. You didn't need to make foundations for roads. You just leveled the ground so it was smooth for a road and there was your road. It was on bedrock at ground level. You didn't need to dig down to bedrock. The bedrock was the surface. It was very convenient for buildings, bad for growing things.

The worst thing was the slight wind due to the atmosphere project that caused a little wind. There was some dust, but because every bit of Ganymede that was not cultivated was rock, the wind just blew the dust to the cultivated land and it usually settled there in the crops or the grasses. Every farmer knew and took great pains to be sure that every bit of ground was scientifically managed and cultivated. If the ground did not have a cash crop growing on it, it at least had grass growing on it that held the soil with its roots. That grass was planted there to prepare the soil for further enrichment. Soil was too precious of a commodity to let it blow away. This was not only basic science, but common knowledge off world (off earth). You learned this at your mother and father's knees or you didn't live long on your own. If you let your dirt blow away or if you don't take care of it, you don't have any and then where do your crops grow.

I want to get back to the topic I started on a little earlier. The way governments run. Well, each world, moon, colony, governed itself. Fortunately, before Earth was successful enough to seed the stars with people, Earth finally cleaned up its own act. The Reform Act of 2096 provided for a unified world government. Each country could keep its own laws and govern their own people. However, certain powers and duties were turned over to the world government to regulate. Among those things were world health, the environment, coining of money, defense of territorial jurisdictions and taxation. Thus each governing authority could tax each area, citizen, company or whatever, only once on each dollar earned or spent.

It went something like this. Each country could tax either income or spending, not both, only once and that was limited by ten percent. The world government was given ten percent and local government, whether state and local counties, etc. could only tax you ten percent. All consumable food and medicines were exempt from taxation. Also all professional fees paid to doctors, lawyers, etc. were exempt. Most countries chose to tax spending as then its citizens could save lots of money and that money saved would be exempt from all taxation until spent. Thus, you paid tax on what you spent and not on what you made. No more underground economy where people escaped from paying taxes because you didn't report income or were paid cash. If you spent it, you paid the tax on it. You didn't get paid to bring children in the world. You had children because you wanted them. If you could not afford them, then nobody paid you to have them.

This may seem like a lot of taxes, but in reality it is not. Most income taxes for people making a living wage used to be a high percentage. I read about this in the United States, where I am from originally. Once you made enough to pay income taxes, you usually paid at a rate of 25 to 39% in income taxes. In some higher income classes, you paid as much as 80 and sometimes 95 percent of your income in taxes. Who would work then? So if you were in a lower tax class, you usually paid at least 33 percent in income tax. You paid sales tax on items you purchased of about 9 or 10 percent. Then you paid social security tax in the USA of 7 ½ percent and if you were self employed you paid about 15 percent. There was also a medicare tax for health insurance, but only used if you were of the retirement age. If you add all this up, you paid right there about 58 ½ percent of your income in taxes. Plus, if you bought some luxury items you paid additional luxury taxes. Then local governments had property taxes on your home. That could equal as much as 5 percent of the value of your home EACH YEAR. I heard that some people were paying more in property taxes to support school systems than they had to pay to repay loans for the purchase of their houses.

I am using the good old USA as a standard only because I am familiar with that standard for 400 years ago. Then some states had a state income tax so that a person ended up paying taxes of over 60% of their income. However, it is no better or worse than any other government. Some things were better and of course some aspects were worse. First, the world government provided for space travel and defense of each country's territories. It is hard to declare war upon yourself. There were no problems with crossing territorial lines when a citizen had the right to live anywhere he could afford to live. Each person was registered upon their birth and they were a charge upon the world government not upon local government. The world government got 10 percent of gross sales revenues for administering the world government, space flight, defense of the countries, and all of their expenses. The countries got ten percent for their governments and local governments got ten percent for all local and regional (state or however they were organized.) Thus the total taxation was not more than 30 percent of money spent. Localities got not more than 1 percent of property values each year for whatever purposes they wanted to use it for. Thus, if you owned a house valued at $100,000 standard dollars, your local government got to tax you up to an extra $1,000 per year on that property. That was, of course, up to the local government.

Another secret in streamlining government was that the people and the government realized that companies could not vote, could not lobby the government, didn't pay taxes and could not contribute to government elections. Each person who declared themselves for public office was given the same amount of free time to campaign. It mattered not who won because each person had the same health care paid for by tax dollars as they had as an elected official, the same retirement paid for by tax dollars and the same benefits. Each citizen of Earth got the same education and all the same benefits. If you wanted more, you had to set it aside. Being a part of the government carried with it no additional benefits or prestige. However, a person could work harder and amass more money for extra things they might want or need. You could buy additional health benefits and retirement benefits. You paid for them yourself. Being a member of government, the government didn't pay for them. Your employer didn't pay for them.

Also when the world government put in the severe penalties for malfeasance in government or public office, it was the first time in history that the penalties greatly reduced the incentive for crimes. People were never tried in courts in their own locality or even country. Thus it did not do a criminal any good to plead that he did good for his voters. That would naturally mean that he did bad things against the voters where he was being tried. Also a person could hold a public or government office only twice. Then he was barred for life from holding that office again.

Corporations and companies were barred from making political contributions or making gifts or any such things. Corporations were not taxed on their income, but paid taxes on their expenditures. Every merchant had to have an electronic cash register tied into the world computer network. It reported the taxes, collected the money electronically and paid it to the merchant's account and the taxing authorities at the moment of sale. At first merchants were inclined to try to get around the system. However, once the government let it be known that anyone turning in a merchant with proof that the merchant did not give an electronic receipt, would get a reward. Then the practice of trying to get around the system dropped dramatically. Now it is a rare occasion that the charge is even brought up. Usually it is a glitch in the machinery. All machines have the electronic codes printed on the receipts and they are issued by the world tax accounting offices located in each country and branches in every locality. They also tied into the country and local databases and the taxes for each are collected at the same time. All that is done and calculated and collected in real time through wireless systems. You could be on the beach on a remote island and they have an electronic uplink to the system for the drinks they sell you at the pool. If they don't want to be bothered, then the drinks are free or a part of the price of the room. Believe me, it is cheaper to give you the drink than to sell you one for a dollar, and not be able to give you a receipt. The penalties are severe. That has caused a lot of merchants to revise their business practices. Hotels charge a flat fee and the drinks at the pool for the guests are free. Other patrons have to go to the payment counter or show a prepaid ticket for that day with the tax already paid. They are now experimenting with a prepaid tax card where you prepay the taxes and then the cash card can be used only once. However, they are still trying to get the bugs out of it. The problem is that they have a very simple and workable system and cash cards sounds like cash money, which we already have. However, it would be cash money that the tax has been prepaid and it could then encourage an underground economy in prepaid tax cash. They you are right back to the same problem of no receipt electronically printed. I don't think it would ever work.

You can, however, give away anything you want. You have to print a receipt for it, but it is free and the receipt says so. I don't mean that you have to print a receipt for a soda that you give away. If a company gives away a car as a prize, they print a receipt for that and they can give it away. There is no tax on that as the company when they bought the car to give it away, paid the tax. You register the winner or recipient. If it is ever called into question as some form of payoff, the records are there to be examined. Computers are good at spotting irregularities. As to that world senator who said it was a coincidence that he and his family members won seven different major prizes that one year and at least 5 other prizes in the next four years, the world court didn't buy that argument and neither did the jury. Like they said, he could have donated them to charity or some worth while purpose and not kept them for their own private use. Plus, the system wide near perfection of the reliability indicators ended all that lying that everyone did. The judge and the jury were not bound to follow the meters, but the public display of the large meters anytime someone was giving testimony was usually enough to discourage lying.

There is no great struggle to avoid paying taxes on income. Income is not taxed. Only the spending of income is taxed. People for years argued that taxing spending such as a sales tax was a regressive tax and only taxed the poor. Well, when you consider that you exempted food and things such as doctors and professional services, I fail to see what is the problem. Sure rich people spend less of a percentage of their income on food. The food they purchase is usually more expensive. All clothing is taxed so you can dress as richly as you want or as poorly. However, since you are paying about one half of the taxes you would normally pay on your income, does it really matter. Rich people pay more or spend more on housing, but so what. All housing is taxed spending. Not at the time you purchase the house. The materials going into the house were taxed when the builder bought them. You indirectly pay tax for your house note or your rent. The landlord pays a percentage of the rent received when it is spent. The mortgage company pays a tax when the company or the employees spend their wages on things. The stockholders of a company pay tax on the money they receive as dividends when they spend that money on things they buy. Companies pay taxes on the things they purchase for the company. Companies are not taxed on income. Companies are not taxed on profits, not are they taxed on money distributed as salaries or as dividends.

Just as I was thinking this through, enough time had passed for the shuttle to dock with the Galo. I hurried off and found my compartment. I was home and missed the old girl. I hadn't been gone from Earth more than a few weeks and already I had fucked my way across the sky. I wasn't complaining, but two marriage proposals in about four weeks was more than I could understand. I almost got a sore back from patting myself on the back so hard. My ego was getting too big, I thought. It was going to get me into trouble.

The ship cast off, that is ship talk for left orbit, about six standard hours later. The next stop would have been Mars, but Mars was still too close to the Sun for a good orbit, so we set our course for the Moon. Yes, I know the shortest distance between two points is a straight line, but that straight line for Mars brought us too close to the Sun right now. After we stopped at the moon, Mars would be next. It would be in a more favorable position then. Normally the orbit of Jupiter would keep us far enough away from the orbit of the Sun to go to Mars, but that was just a quirk of the positioning of the planets at this time. No deep political or scientific implications or anything, just a fact of life based on the relative positions of the planets.

Two days after we got underway, Gert wanted to go see the new movie. Well, I was sufficiently recovered and accepted the date. It was a new comedy that had been beamed to the ship from Earth and was highly rated. It turned out to be good. We had a nice time and Gert wanted again to show me the new heavens from this position in space. Of course I accepted. We fell into each other's arms and kissed upon entering the compartment anteroom. I had fortunately brought my lubrication so that there were no awkward moments, and Gert let me know that he was ready. He had also fortunately brought with him a jacket that doubled as a pillow and blanket. We lay there in each other's arms and studied the sky and talked and kissed. We took turns sucking on each other and finally he asked me to fuck him again.

"Put your love inside of me again. I love to feel you ...fucking away inside of me and making me feel good inside of me. From my toes to the top of my head I feel you moving inside of me and it gives me great pleasure." With this I kissed him again and I lifted his legs over my head and put them on my shoulders. I bent over and kissed and licked his hole and entered him with my tongue. I then leaned up and kissed him with the same lips that had kissed his hole and he licked my lips to taste me and indirectly himself. I lubricated my organ and entered him slowly. We fucked for a long time and I concentrated of giving the greatest amount of pleasure I knew how to Gert. When I could tell that his body was experiencing multiple periods of intense pleasure, I asked him if he was ready to have his climax.

"Yes. Any time. Please cum. I don't know how much longer I can stand this pleasure without crying out for release from this torture of ecstasy. I want you to kiss me while I experience you pumping yourself inside of me. Hurry. Please. I can't take anymore." I kissed him and reached down and grabbed him and the skin around his dick and moved my hand back and forth over him and it was over just that quick for him. I pumped back and forth inside of him, but it was over for him and just as quickly it was over for me. We lay there locked in our embraces and had a wonderful time. We spent the time kissing, licking, nipping and playing with our mouths with each other.

About ten minutes later, we lay there cuddled in each other's arms. I took the blanket he brought and spread it on top of us. I awoke later to his back side backed up to me and my arms around him. I entered him again and we lay there spooning together. We were joined by my dick in his ass hole. After a while, he started moving and I asked him if he was uncomfortable.

"No. I want you to fuck me again." I started to move back and forth and over the next hour I started and stopped multiple times. Finally I reached in front of Gert and held him in my hand and gently massaged his dick and continued to fuck him. He finally turned around a little, and we kissed again. Then he consciously tightened up his hole. I pumped some more, and both he and I came. He spilled his seed into my hand and I spilled my seed into his hole. I brought my hand up and he licked his seed from my hand. I held him for a long time, just content to hold such a nice caring person in my arms and loving on him. Later he said that perhaps we had better get back to our quarters. The movie had ended six hours ago. People would start to wonder where we were if we were gone any longer.

We got dressed, kissed again and then left about ten minutes apart. We went to different parts of the ship and made sure that we arrived back at our quarters at least ten minutes apart to get to our bunks to sleep before the next duty shift.

The next day, I was exhausted. I think so was Gert. I felt wonderful, but tired from all that extracurricular activities. What a way to go. Fucked yourself to death. Don't laugh. Better than dying of terminal hornies. That is not a pleasant condition either. I know and so does any M-W or M-M man. When a man wants to fuck he will find something to fuck, even if it is just his fist or his sleeping pad. If it doesn't have a hole, he will make a hole in it to fuck. The only reason they make ships out of steel is that is the only thing harder than a space man's dick in times of need. In the old wooden ships I guess the sailor with the bunk with the best knot hole in his bunk was the luckiest sailor who had the most popular bunk. I guess knot holes were popular, otherwise sailors would be fucking holes in the ship everywhere. I read somewhere that sailors had an old saying about what they did when they were out to sea. When in port their ships would be tied up to a pier. While out to sea, there were no women on those old time ships hundreds of years ago. They were all phobic about doing something with another man, that was called queer. But they used to say that it wasn't queer unless you were tied to the pier. Meaning if you fucked each other that was fine as long as you were not in port and could not get a woman. But if you were in port and could get a woman, then to do it with another guy was queer. Hey, a hole's a hole and the sex of the hole doesn't change if you are out to sea or at the pier. But if that is how you want to justify it, who am I to question.

I have to confess. I don't care what you do. I don't care who you do it with. Just enjoy it and make sure it is with consenting adults. With the age of consent being 16 system wide, almost all persons are adults when they are physically old enough to engage in or perform sex. Sure they don't always have the emotional maturity, but I know some people who are 25 that don't have the emotional maturity. Yes, the older you are, the more emotional maturity you have. However, does that mean that you can put off giving a person their right to consent to sex until they are mature enough. The debates on Earth are brought up over and over again. The answer is the same. The authorities, the police or whatever you call the local law enforcement do not want to have to hunt down and prosecute people for engaging in consensual sexual acts. They don't care if the person is 150 years old or 18 years old. If you are old enough to do it voluntarily, then you are old enough to consent.

Perhaps that is why we monitor marriage and fertility so closely. You can marry someone, anyone you want of just about any age. You can also get a divorce, but you are still responsible for them to some extent. If you can consent to it, it is not rape. Today, the government will get you a woman or a man if you want one. The government health system will pay for a paid professional sex therapist for at least one session a month for anyone. Just go and apply. There is no need to rape anyone. You can't sell what others are giving away. For those sick people who consider rape a sex act, they just don't get it. The sick people who rape other people do it for power and control over them. Rape is an act of violence against another person, not a sex act. Sex is just the method they use to prove or demonstrate their power over that other person.

Once the scientists developed the reliability indicators (actually meters) around 2120, testifying in court became a big deal. Nobody can ever tell you for certain that you are lying or telling the truth, but with the advances in forensics and the reliability indicator meters, court hearings and trials became more of a search for the truth and a telling of your story instead of a swearing match.

Chapter Nine

A couple of days later Joel wanted a return match. I figured, why not. We made plans to spend the entire off duty shift in his communications room. We brought refreshments with us, some snacks and blankets and other supplies. We each had some off duty time and set it up to run at the same time. While no one knew what was up, we still kept it low key. I was beginning to realize that there were so many places on board ship for people to meet privately because I believe the designers set it up that way. A crew man who spends his off duty time fucking his brains out, is not spending his off duty time getting into trouble and certainly doesn't want to upset the apple cart. He just wants to keep getting laid regularly. For that reason the ship I am beginning to suspect is loaded with places for secret liaisons or meetings and sexual trysts. Not adulterous affairs, just sexual affairs between consenting adults who are free to frolic as they see fit. For all I knew at any one time about one third the ship was fucking their brains out, a third was on duty and the other third was sleeping. The rest of the time the thirds just rotated their turns and waited for their turn to get their brains fucked out. Well, maybe not quite that many, but a good percentage and probably over 25 percent or more of the off duty people at any one time were engaged in sex or mutual physical play. Given a few weeks together, people will sort out who wants to fuck or suck whom. And invariably, people will somehow pair off and sort themselves out. Let me state this in an obviously simpler way. A hard dick will find a willing hole. That's about as simple as I can put it. I assume that we have some W-W women and couples. I just have not met any of them, but you know, committed people do not advertise their sexuality. They do not need to and unless you are interested in having sex with them, it simply is none of anyone's business.

We made arrangements for one entire day to get ready and we met an hour after we got off duty assignments. Neither of us were due back for at least 16 hours. Joel had this room to himself for that time. All communication relief officers had their own communications room and would not need to use this room unless there was a system failure. Then they would page Joel to get in. The only exception is if the ship hits a meteor (actually vice versa) and we lose most of the crew and the survivors make it to this communications room. Rather far fetched I believe. The communications room had a food and beverage cooler built in and a port for movies. He even had a small microwave heater for food and beverages. However, the movie port was dead during the watch periods. Since Joel was not on watch, he could tap into the ship's signal.

This was like having our own private bedroom with a sleeping platform. Not very big, but when you are huddled together, who needs big and luxurious. Just further that you have to chase your loved one to find his naked body. You just need privacy. As much as I liked sex, I was not interested in putting on a public show. I didn't even want anyone to know what I was up to. To tell you the truth, they didn't want to know and they were probably off trying to do the same thing in their spare time. We started out sipping some wine and eating a sandwich we had brought with us from the mess room. We turned out the lights and watched a movie and talked and ate and drank. We just had a good time being with each other. We undressed about half way into the movie and lay there under the covers on the sleeping platform. I didn't bring my holographic recorder because Joel being a communications officer would know what that was. Besides, I had gotten over the infantile compulsion to record my encounters for later enjoyment by me of my different companions. I had outgrown my need to relive my conquests. I had only had sex with one person before I met John. John was the second. Gert was the third. Joel was the fourth and my unidentified friend whose name I found out when I checked my personal pad was named Cyryl, or Cy for short, was the fifth. I had only had sex with 5 different people in my entire 20 years. Up until about three months ago, I had only had sex with one person my entire life.

I guess it is true that the first person that you fuck usually is the first person to win your heart. I probably would not have had sex with so many other people except that Tobert had moved on and there is such excellent man flesh all around me that it keeps me in a constant state of arousal. I want to fuck every cute guy I see. For some strange reason, just about every guy has some characteristic about him that seems to make him cute to me at the time. I don't know if I am just plain horny or if the greater my horny condition begets the lower standards of attractiveness. I thought about that and then I realized that I found a great variety of men attractive, but the people I chose to be intimate with were all very nice people and I truly enjoyed my time with each of them. Any one of them would be very fine people to be married to if I ever wanted to be married. Fortunately, I just didn't want to be married to anyone

We were both tired from our duty watch and we agreed to rest before we did anything. We held each other and slept for a few hours. Our bellies were full of food and wine and we had watched a good movie. It was nice to fall asleep in the arms of a man. We hugged and we kissed, then we fell asleep. I awoke to Joel sucking on my tit and holding me. I don't know if he was fully awake, but obviously he was enjoying himself. I held him close and fell asleep again. The next time I awoke, he was lower and sucking on my dick. I just let him suck away and drifted back to sleep. Some time later I awoke to find Joel urinating into a small urinal built into the communications room wall. Perhaps five hours had passed from the time we had turned off the movie. We had been here almost 8 hours and yet to have sex. It was nice; the pressure was off of us to have sex on a schedule. When Joel finished, I got up and used the urinal for myself. We sat back down on the platform. We were both naked and we grabbed each other. We had not been under any pressure to have sex, but now we both wanted it and were under the pressure of our own desires. I looked at him and marveled at such a fine specimen of manhood. He was small, but manly in his own way and he was the only person I had met with a dick bigger than my own.

We hugged and kissed and held each other and then we turned and assumed a 69 position and performed oral sex on each other. This was so mutually satisfying that within minutes, I felt his massive organ become even bigger and more clear fluid flowed from his penis and began to drive me wild with desire. I loved the taste of him. Within minutes we each filled the other's mouth with our essential bodily fluid, the substance of life and the great divider of the sexes. The thing that separated the men from the boys. The boys did not produce sperm and the men did. We eagerly shared that special distinction of what we produced with each other. Giving to the other a copious amount of our essence, we kissed again. We sharred a mouth full of that frothy white cream for the other to suck down and swallow and enjoy.

When it was over, we just stayed there and continued to suck on each other. We each had laid our heads on the legs of the other and closed our eyes. I kept nursing on his dick for a long time. When I awoke later his dick was again hard in my mouth as mine was in his. This time we sucked slower and after a while we both came up for air. He looked at me and told me the sweetest words that another man can hear. "I want you to fuck me again. I want you to fuck me like you did the last time. I want to feel you hit that special spot you found last time and I want you to fuck my brains out. I have been able to think of nothing else since you did that last time."

"Your wish is my command. I will fuck you until you scream uncle."

"What somebody's uncle got to do with this?"

"Sorry, just another old Earth slang term. It means until you give up and beg me to stop."

"Well, I don't think we have that much time. As far as I am concerned, as long as it feels good you can fuck me all you want. But I must warn you that I do want a return bout. If not today, then the next time.'

"No you don't. You don't want a return bout, you just want me to be mad enough at you to fuck your brains out and to keep fucking you so that I won't stop until we both have to go back on duty again. That's what you want, I think."

"No. It is not. Well, let me restate that. I want that and then I want to fuck you too."

"Well, you can't have both, because we don't have enough time."

"We can make the time."

"In your dreams."

"Yes. I made the time there for you for the last two weeks. Now I want you for real." We kissed and I reached over and put the lubricant on myself and then on his hole. I eased myself into him and within minutes he was relaxed enough to allow me to move back and forth inside of him. I moved around and varied the angle. Then I felt him relax and I struck his secret spot and his eyes opened and he moaned. I thrust again and I had hit him again in that spot. If I kept it up it would feel unbelievably good and he would let me fuck him into the next century without stopping. Such is the power of a man fucking the right man in the right spot. It is not to be understood until it has been experienced. We kept up our fucking for perhaps an hour or more. I would periodically slow down or speed up. Sometimes I would stop and wait so that I would not cum and spoil his pleasure. Finally I could hold off no longer and as I neared my climax, I bent down and took his large dripping organ in my mouth. I sucked on him and waited for him to again fill my mouth with his seed. I always like to climax after the man I am fucking. Once I cum, I can no longer continue to fuck. Then the man may not experience his orgasm if I lose my hardness. They tell me that for people who like to get fucked they really enjoy experiencing their climax while being fucked or with a hard dick in their ass.

I wanted to give him all the pleasure he deserved and desired. I made sure that he shot his seed into my mouth and then I shared it with him as I furiously pumped mine into his eager hole. He bucked and squirmed underneath me and that made it more fun to ride his ass. He was enjoying it and told me so. He urged me on to fuck him. Of course, I did until I came too. We laid there. Two thoroughly satisfied people. I held him in my arms and kissed him and held him to me. We rested, and then I closed my eyes and fell asleep.

We awoke to a small alarm about two hours later. Joel had set an alarm to let us know that we only had about 6 hours left. He told me that now he wanted to spend some time giving me pleasure. I immediately became suspicious.

"Don't worry I am not going to fuck you."

"What do you want to do?"

"I want to use my finger inside of you to give you the pleasure that you gave me the first time. I will only use one finger, but I want to find your spot and give you the pleasure that you gave me. I want to learn how to give that kind of pleasure to a man."

"That's all right. You don't need to do that to me."

"I know it's all right and I don't have to, but I want to suck on you and play with your ass hole and learn how to give you pleasure."

"But then you will want to fuck me and I don't want you to try and put your big thing inside of me. It is just too big."

"I promise you all I want to do is to learn how to please you. I can not describe how good it feels, but I want to learn where it is and how to find it. Please let me put my finger in you." How could I resist? It was only a finger and I had fucked him several times.

"Okay. But only a finger." He reached for my tube of lubrication. I lay back down in the dim room and allowed him to feel around and find my hole. I then directed him. "First, you must not rush this. You smear the lubrication all around my hole and gradually work a little of it into my hole with your finger. Your finger will become dry with lubrication and you must withdraw it and smear it around again outside my hole. Again and again you must do this just slightly into my hole and then out and around my hole again and again. Each time, wetting your finger with the lubricant around my hole. Then wet it AGAIN with the lubrication there. You do this over and over again and each time your finger will gain a little more entrance. If you rush it, it will hurt the person and not feel good. If this takes fifteen standard minutes, then that is what it takes. You have to rub your finger around my hole as that feels good to the person you are rubbing." He was an eager student. He shifted his position to be more comfortable.

"Is this good. Am I doing it right."

"Yes. But don't listen to me because any other person is not going to be able to talk you through this. They could, but they won't. If you don't know how to make love to an ass hole, then you don't deserve to play with one or be allowed to put your finger in one. You have to be extremely sensitive and acutely aware of your lover. I say lover, because not just anyone will let you put you finger up their ass hole. And for you to do it and for it not to hurt, you have to win that person's complete trust. From my point of view, I am not going to open up to you. You have to tease my hole, lubricate my hole and play with my hole such that my hole wants to open up for you."

"You make this too difficult."

"No. I don't."

"Why do you like me to fuck you?"

"Because it feels good."

"And why does it feel good."

"Just because it does."

"Wrong answer. It feels good because I love your ass hole and I want your hole to let me crawl up in there. I don't take advantage of your hole. I make love to it. And then it wants me. You have to want

118

to please me more than yourself and then my hole will want your finger inside of it. You are more concerned how to get your finger in my hole and not how to make my hole want your finger. You are being selfish."

"You are just making this difficult."

"I am telling you why you love my finger up inside of your hole and you are arguing with me. Then you don't need me. Stick your own finger up your own hole."

"I tried that and it didn't feel good."

"That's my point. Do it my way and then it will feel good to me. Otherwise just let me fuck you again and admit you are not patient enough to convince my ass hole to let you in because you want to make love to it. Right now you just want to stick you finger up my ass hole as if that proves something. How sad a situation for you, and how unpleasant a thing for me."

"Okay. You win. I will do it your way."

"You want to make love to me, then don't do it begrudgingly." I reached up and brought his head to mine. "Now lover just following my directions and I will love what you are doing to me."

"How do you know?"

"Because it worked on you." I looked at him and smiled. "Now keep teasing my hole and put a little more lubrication on your finger and my hole. It doesn't take much." He did that and for the next ten minutes he moved his finger around and entered me slightly and then withdrew. Over and over again he did this and more and more lubrication was around my hole. Then on one gentle push, his finger entered past my anal muscle. He was inside of me and he moved his finger around a little.

"See. When you had teased it and made love to it enough, it willingly opened up to receive you."

"Yes. I noticed, that and when I stopped trying to push inside of you, I gradually got more and more of my finger inside of you and your hole. It gradually opened up to receive me. Did I hurt you?"

"No. You took your time, you made love to my hole and I wanted you. I loved the feel of you paying attention to me through my hole. Now move your finger around slowly and move it back and forth in a fucking motion, but do not pull in all the way out. Feel around and if you go to about where the back of my dick is located in my ass hole, do you feel a slight bump or hard spot?"

"No. Not yet." Over and over again he moved around and gave me some pleasure. Then he felt something and on the next inward movement he struck it again. "Yes. I feel something."

"Well, stop the fucking motion or make it more shallow. Don't pull out so much. Keep you finger mostly inside of me, but move it back and forth and gently rub that spot."

"Yes. I can feel it. It seems to pulse and get bigger and move as I rub it."

"Well, you have to be very careful, but that is a man's pleasure spot and if you rub it gently or when you fuck him you bump and rub it with your dick, you can bring great pleasure to him." He leaned over and took my dick in his mouth. He sucked on me and rubbed me from the inside and I could feel that I poured fluid like a leaky faucet.

Joel kept this up for perhaps a half hour and I loved the feeling he was causing in my hole and then sucking on my dick, I was in heaven if it existed. When he stopped, I felt cheated as I had not yet had my climax. "Are you tired. Are you quitting?"

"No. But I have to change my position. Did it feel good to you?"

"Of course it did, or I would have asked you to stop a long time ago."

"I am learning so much from you about sex."

"You are not learning anything from me about sex; I hope that you are learning about love. I don't teach sex. I like to think that we are loving each other and not just having sex." I laid on my side and we resumed a modified position. Joel was now on his side and he put more lubrication on his hand and then sucked my dick into his mouth. I opened my legs to give him greater access to my hole. He entered me again with his finger and then I felt another finger trying to gain entrance. "If your second finger wants entrance, he is going to have to do the same thing. Make love to my hole and when my hole wants him in, then he will be able to gain entrance. He kept this up for more time and eventually he opened me up for two fingers. He kept up rubbing my spot and several times I thought I was going to cum, but each time he kept up the rubbing, but only held me in his mouth and stopped the movements.

Within a half hour he had a third finger trying to gain entrance. Finally he had three fingers inside of me. I knew what was coming next.

"I want to fuck you. I want to make love to your body like you did to mine and to bring you the same pleasure that you brought to me." He looked me in the eye. "Will you please let me fuck you?"

I didn't say a thing. I didn't stop him, but I didn't say a thing. He kissed me again and he pushed ever so gently his tongue into my mouth. He was trying to claim me as his and to fuck both my mouth and my ass hole at the same time. I didn't say no and he took that as consent. He reached down and put lubrication on his mighty tool and then guided himself to my hole. He teased my hole with his dick just like he did with his fingers. Over and over again he pushed the head in a little. Over and over again he smeared the head around my hole to get more lubrication on the head of his dick. Then finally after twenty minutes or so he gained entrance into me. It hurt like a mother fucker, (another old Earth slang word) but I also wanted it. He had teased my hole and worked me up to it where I wanted him to fuck me.

Gradually he started to move back and forth and with each stroke he gained more and more entrance into me. It still hurt, but it was becoming a good hurt. Within minutes he had gotten the entire length of himself inside of me. "Now move around," I told him. "You have to find the right spot and the right angle to stimulate me. Lean back a little to change the angle and get the head of your dick to rub my insides. Now a little deeper. Right about there. Can you feel it. That is the spot. Pretty soon, you will be able to find it on your own. Right there, now fuck me lover. Fuck my brains out and make me cum."

Joel huffed and puffed and fucked for the longest time. He had cum about two times and been fucked by me for at least an hour and this time his nut was going to be a long time in arriving. But that was all right, his dick hurt me so bad and yet felt so good at the same time. I crossed my eyes and let him do all the work of fucking me into pleasure. Over and over, again and again, the waves of pleasure swept through my body. I could not climax, but it felt like I was close to cuming and that I was having a miniature orgasm over and over again. I was in sheer ecstasy and enjoying every inch of it. Finally I stopped concentrating on my orgasm and just laid there and let him fuck me into oblivion. It felt wonderful and I wanted the feeling to continue for a long time. I remembered how big his dick was and was certain that I would walk funny for about a week after this was over. I also was afraid that I would be so numb back there that I may shit on myself after this is over. However, with the feeling of how great this felt, I just didn't care at this moment.

I pulled his face to mine and let him invade my mouth again and I saw the sweat on his body. I was lying there enjoying this immensely and he was working up a sweat. I turned my head and chewed on his neck. I nibbled on his ear and I lightly bit his ear lobe. He was sweating up a storm. I lifted one of his arms. I don't even remember which one and buried my face in his pit and sucked his sweat directly from his underarm. He had as much hair there, it seemed, as he had on his head. It smelled of him and I inhaled his fragrance and became even more sexually aroused if that was possible. Joel was such a fucking sexy little thing with such a big thing that I became even harder. I loved the feel of his belly hair rubbing against me and rubbing my dick. With each thrust into my ass hole as he bent over me fucking my ass, his belly hair rubbed against my dick as a gentle stimulation that kept me excited along with his big fucking dick rubbing me from the inside. I later measured it one day with him and it was every bit of 24 cm in length and 14 cm around. This little boy was a big boy. I was on the verge of cuming. But it just wasn't enough to get me off.

Over and over again he fucked into me. I hovered at the brink of my climax. When next I glanced over at the clock, I noticed that we had been fucking for just short of two hours. A new record for me and I know if must be for him. I had never before been fucked and from the way he was doing this, I think that he had never fucked before. The truth was I had never been fucked before. I know that he had never fucked like this before. Because if he had, his ego would have been impossible to deal with. As it was, he knew that he had probably the biggest dick on the ship and I had decided that after fucking him for an hour several times to let him inside my poor ass hole. I changed my mine right then and there. I was glad I let him in me. It felt better than I could ever could have imagined it would, and I was so happy letting my stud fuck me that I didn't care about the pain and regret of tomorrow. Mark my words; I knew that I was going to have regrets tomorrow. I didn't know if it would be because I couldn't handle his superior attitude as a result of letting him fuck me and the fact that I liked it; or just the fact that I would be as sore as a virgin bride after her honeymoon, and he would lord it over me. I was prepared for the worst. I didn't know what it would be, but I had already mentally prepared for it.

I could tell that finally he was getting close to cuming. I could feel his dick growing even bigger. Believe me, if his dick grew an extra layer of skin, I would have felt it. There wasn't any extra space in my ass hole for anything. So any change in him, I instantly felt directly by my senses. He leaned over and raised my arm and started sucking on my arm pits. First he sucked on one arm pit, then the other arm pit. He had to lean over more to do this, and this caused his belly to come in closer contact with mine. That put more pressure on my dick and increased the friction between his hairy belly and my dick. He humped me like nothing before and then I could feel his dick expand and pulse his life seeds into me. Over and over again I felt him pulse as he held steady inside of me. I counted them. 5,.... 6,.... 7,.... 8,.... 9,.... 10,.... Then he pulled back al little and he slammed into me one final time and stopped.

"Quick. Take me in your mouth and let me cum in your mouth." He leaned up a little and took my throbbing organ in his mouth and sucked up and down on it and that was all it took. Again and again I pulsed in his mouth and filled it full of my sperm and got my heaven sent release. He stayed on my dick and wouldn't let go. I just lay back and my entire body went limp. He held me in his mouth which was warm and soft and kind to my battered body. Then it happened so fast I had no control over it. My bladder cut loose as I had been holding inside of me some piss and now that my body was totally relaxed, some escaped. It flowed directly into Joel's mouth. He drank it down and smiled at me. I got control over my body and he looked up at me and held my dick in his hand and asked.

"Why did you stop?"

"Do you want me to pee in your mouth?"

"You are my lover. I will do anything to please you."

"Yes, but is that what you want?"

"I love the taste of you." So I laid back and released my golden yellow flow. Not my idea of sex, but I would do anything at this point to please my lover right now. I didn't have much because we had just gone before we started this last sex marathon session. I gave him what I had because he wanted it. Joel drank it down and smiled at me. He came up to my face and we kissed. I could taste my pee in his mouth and he ran his tongue around the inside of my mouth. Joel was the hottest, sexiest little fucker on this ship. I just don't think I would be up to this but perhaps once a lunar or even less. Joel was only 18 years old and I was 20. What have I done, I fell for a younger man.

"We better get dressed because we have to hit the showers before we go on duty." I told him. He lifted his arm and sniffed his pit.

"A little ripe, but you cleaned most of it out with your tongue."

"Then here, let me get the rest." With that I lifted his arm and started licking his arm pit and tasted his fragrance and it made me horny again. He lifted my arm and did the same. We continued this mutual pit admiration society for a while and then we continued dressing. I looked up at him slightly as I was still seated and he was standing. He was so sexy and good looking that my heart was melting. I reached over and pulled his underwear open and pulled his dick out and sucked him into my mouth and cleaned him off. He started getting hard again and I quickly put him back into his underwear. I couldn't handle him again this soon.

"You need to learn to keep that thing under control. You are lucky that you don't have to register it as a dangerous weapon and store it while on board ship."

"You know where I would like to store it every day."

"Well, I have one that you can store for me daily too." I looked at him. I really didn't want to continue this conversation because I knew where it was going. I didn't want it to go there. I was not ready to settle down nor did I want to declare myself and Joel an M-M couple and get private quarters. There were just too many places onboard ship to conduct activities in private that you didn't need to get separate quarters unless you wanted to get married and settle down. I could see why most M-M couples kept to their private quarters. They were comfortable and they had their life and were very happy with their life. They didn't associate with us except during work because they just didn't care about us unless you were just social friends with one of them.

It wasn't until the next off loading that I grew to know one member of an M-M couple. I will tell you about that later. Joel and I left about ten minutes apart. He let me out and I went to my quarters. I got my shower stuff and went to the G gym. I did a light workout to explain the sweat and tiredness, and then we took a steam bath together. That was where I met up with Joel. We acted like we didn't know each other except in passing and said hi and that was it. In the steam room I made sure I rinsed out my abused hole thoroughly to ease any pain and suffering. I saw that Joel did the same. I had forgotten that I had fucked the shit out of him before he fucked me. I was so sore I had forgotten about Joel. There was no one in the room when I left and I turned to Joel, kissed him quickly and patted his leg and left to shower again.

Chapter Ten

We both, Joel and I, had 8 hour duty assignments today. Normally you have only 4 hour duty assignments and then at least another 4 hours before your next shift. However, once every 14 days, the first duty assignment and the last are back to back and then you do a straight 8 hour shift. Actually, just two 4 hour shifts back to back. There was no time for a meal so then you were allowed to bring a snack with you and to go to the head a couple of times provided you had a relief to cover for you. In my duty station, I was always junior to everyone so I covered for everyone and they just let me go whenever I needed it as long as all the other men were all on duty. This is more of a safety precaution than a necessity. Because I filled in on each duty station, I had actual experience at every duty station. They routinely ran training drills for me at each station. I was becoming pretty proficient at every station and I actually loved the challenges. However, today everyone worked 8 straight hours and the drills were kept to a minimum to keep everyone sharp and ready. I was given training tapes to watch and play on the training console. This was a dummy control console that could substitute as a backup for any console but its primary purpose was to run training lessons and drills for me, the intern. It also was used to teach the crew members new procedures and equipment upgrades. They also got periodic performance testing on this console. So this console was as modern as all the others. When I got off, I headed back to my bunk and saw Joel headed for his bunk. I awoke several times to hear him snoring lightly and rolled over to resume snoring myself. I drifted off to sleep and thought that life was good even if wore you out.

I was awakened about 6 hours later with a ship wide emergency alert horn sounding. I felt a jerk of the ship and was practically thrown from my bunk despite the partial artificial gravity effect. I know that they can only compensate for a little under one-half G force and in space between a quarter and a half, but it seemed to me that the ship's copilot was doing a sloppy job. We quickly donned our air masks and reported in just our underwear to the emergency duty station by our bunk room. Look, air masks won't save your life in the vacuum of space even if that vacuum occurs inside the compartment of your ship. On the off chance that we lose pressurization because a portion of the ship's hull gets breached by a small meteor or some other problem, then the air mask we donned may give you the few extra seconds to scramble to safety or initiate curative measures. This can be a patch or just plain getting out of that compartment and perhaps saving your bunk mates lives. In this case it was not a practice run, but the approach of a near collision of a small meteor that we just didn't know was there or more likely wasn't supposed to be there.

That is exactly the reason why do don't just dump bodies into space. There is enough stuff out there that can kill you. You don't need to add to the space trash that everyone has to keep up with. The bodies that are sent to the Sun are carefully tracked until they are pulled into the Sun and consumed into the fires of everlasting rebirth as the memorial service says. We studied that at the Academy. I don't know if they try to frighten you away from space travel or are concerned about your immortal soul. They have a deep thread or fiber of belief in something bigger, a creator out there somewhere that is found in the members of the space corps. I think I was beginning to pick it up myself. I couldn't put my finger on it, but when I saw the stars, I mean really saw the stars out there when Gert showed me the observation port, I was impressed. No, I was in awe of the unknown, of the vastness of space and of the immensity of the universe. Then something that the discoverer of the limitation of the speed of light, and Einstein said, came to mind. God does not play dice with the universe. I was beginning to understand what he meant.

We were finally told to stand down after about ten minutes, and the orders came through that a near collision was avoided by the quick action of the crew. That was the acceleration I felt. It wasn't severe because you just don't want to move a few million metric tons of mass too fast. First, you use up too much fuel, and you change your orbit too much and change everything down the road for the rest of the trip unless you can correct to get back on course. Second, and probably more important, If you move the Galo too fast, the ship becomes a lethal weapon to the things inside of the ship. The contents are moving one direction and the ship moving in the other. The damages from that can be worse than what the meteor does to the ship and the occupants.

We were told to stand down and we resumed our normal ship duties. Mine was to finish sleeping. I looked over at Joel; he smiled and winked at me. I was going to have a hard time keeping that boy away from my ass hole, and he was going to have a hard time keeping me away from his beautiful tight little hole. I started getting hard again and put him out of my thoughts. However, I realized that being an M-M couple had advantages. Right now I could be burying my aching hard member deep into my lover's ass hole and knocking off a quick piece of ass while holding him in my arms and kissing him. Then I realized that I couldn't think like that, and I tried to roll over on my stomach and couldn't because something was in the way. Finally I drifted off to sleep.

When my personal alarm went off, I silenced it and decided I could afford to sleep another hour. I didn't have any duty station to be at for another four hours. I had gotten enough of a work out physically with Joel that I counted that as my exercise for the next two off periods. Everyone had already gotten up and left for their stations or to get things done before their next assignment station. Only Joel and I were left. That didn't mean that at any moment someone might not come wandering in, but briefly we were alone. Joel came over to talk to me.

"Time to get up sleepy head."

"I'm too tired. I just want to sleep another hour."

"Well, we could go to my duty station and have 4 hours of privacy where you could just do that I could have my way with you while you slept."

"No. I don't think so. I am still sore and I couldn't sleep with that elephantine thing up inside of me moving around like a battering ram."

"Well, I could just lie there and let you annoy me if you wanted to."

"I want to, but the body is just not able to move enough necessary to do justice to you for about the next couple of hours."

"We each have only a 4 hour duty shift, we could meet afterwards and I could give you a return bout with me sleeping and you doing all the work."

"You are up to that again so soon."

"For you I am. I would be ready every day all day if you wanted me to be ready. I would only put you through what I did today say once or twice a week. We could get quarters together, and then we could always be together and never have to worry about sneaking around. I could hold you in my arms all night long too."

"Are you asking me to marry you."

"No. I don't intend to make an honest man out of you. I just want to keep you for my personal stud service and occasionally lend you out to other crew members."

"You would do that?"

"No, but believe me, they would come to me and ask me for your services after I got done bragging about you. However, I would want to keep you all to myself."

"How kind of you. But right now I don't even think that I can walk right." He looked at me and asked.

"But was it worth it. Did it feel good to you?" He smiled and looked at me with those puppy dog eyes filled with love. "I didn't hurt you did I?"

"Yes, but it was worth it, Yes it felt good. It felt better than anything I had ever felt. Before you ask, yes it hurt." I knew it was a good hurt. "But from now on take your boot off before you stick your foot up my ass hole." I could see that no one had returned to the room so I continued. "I can meet you after our next 4 hour duty. At the last 8 hour shift I thought that I was going to leak shit out my hole and on the console seat. When that didn't happen, I thought I might just sit on the seat and lose it up inside of me. I need time to rest."

"Okay, I will see you after the next shift. Meet me at my communications station. If anyone says anything we are going to see a movie or you can send a communication home or something. Bring some snacks so we don't have to leave. I will get us some too." I promptly went back to sleep for another hour. I awoke and set it for another hour. Thus, when I finally got up I was rested and had only two hours before my next duty assignment. I picked up some beverages and some snack food, nuts, berries, etc. for us to snack on. I put them in a carryalong and went to my duty station in time and was finally awake and ready for duty.

I reviewed the ship's logs and found out that we had a near collision with an unknown piece of space junk. We had dispatched a shuttle vehicle to match orbit and speed with it and bring in on board. The collective space governments offered bounties for all space junk in known orbits. However, least you think this is an open license to get money for picking up junk or just happening to find stuff that wasn't there, think again. Each find had to be verified as to where it came from and if there was no verification and your computer records did not show how you found it on a prefiled flight path, they were very reluctant to pay the bounty. However, something of historic significance that was verified as authentic could pay nice bonuses and incentives to the crew that finds it.

Since we were a quasi military craft, the money went into a fund to help the widows, orphans, and close relatives of the non commissioned crew. The professional military crew members were technically ineligible for any benefits from space junk and other things for doing their duty. The service took care of its own members and family. In this manor we had discretionary funds to take care of our own crew members. The piece of junk was rather large and had been successfully retrieved and the science people were pouring over it. The warning alarm had gone off because it was on a course to possibly intersect with us. However, it was traveling very slowly when compared to most meteors. It was its immense size that attracted attention. The estimate was that it massed about 10 kilos. If that thing had hit us, it could have done immense damage even at a slow velocity.

I need to explain that the kinetic energy of a body in motion, that's anything out there that is moving, depends on its mass and its speed. We use mass, because without gravity nothing has weight, but it always has mass. Trust me; it does. Newton said that everything that moves tends to stay moving and when it hits something then it gives that thing the energy it has and you have to absorb that energy to stop the thing. I am trying to make this simple to understand. Think of it this way. If I throw a bullet at you, it can hit you and then will fall to the ground. A bullet fired from a gun going very fast can go right through you and kill you. So speed is important. The greater the mass of something, the more umph, think of that as weight, it has. You run into your house, you will stop suddenly and you will feel it. If your house is moving as fast as you were walking and it hits you, the house will not stop and you may not ever get up again. The alarm was triggered not because of its speed, but because of its size and therefore indirectly its inferred mass.

If you don't like this explanation, then catch me when I am on my duty shift and I can show you the books that have the formulas and show you the math. It loses something when you take away the numbers and have to just plain explain it in English. I know that earth standard English is actually mostly American English, but the language of space is many times just mathematics. It doesn't translate into any language as well as it expresses an idea in the language of mathematics. On duty I reviewed the logs of all the duty stations from the previous shift and prepared my extracts for the senior duty officer and he compared it to the summaries prepared by the previous shift. He signed my reports and they were filed into the record book. The electronic reports were finalized and stored.

My duty shifts always went fast if I wasn't dragging my feet or as in the last shift my ass because it had been fucked so royally. I was sure of my duties, had learned my responsibilities and all of the consols and really enjoyed my job. I was eager to learn more. I was told my progress report was satisfactory and that I would be getting new duty assignments in the near future for other duty stations that I was to learn. When my shift was over, I gathered up my carryalong and headed to Joel's communication room. I knocked once and he opened the door and let me inside. I laid the carryalong down and got out our provisions for a nice snack. Neither of us had another duty assignment for 12 hours. A nice time for us to have fun and relax together. This was three shifts. We only worked an average of 8 standard hours in a 24 standard hour period. However, sometimes it was 4 on, 4 off 8 resting and then 4 on, 4 off, and 4 on and 12 off. It varied to keep us on our toes and so that everyone could have extended periods of off time together. The ship had basically three shifts for constant manning of all duty stations. Actually, there were four shifts. With the days off rotations and other variables, this enabled everyone to have sufficient time for themselves.

With 12 hours to ourselves, we ate leisurely, watched a movie, lounged around naked on the sleeping platform, and played with each other. We took a nap together and it was the first time since the beanstalk trip up to space, and any free time Tobert and I could spend together that I had to actually sleep with a naked man. I looked over at his naked frame laying next to my body. I was still in awe of his sheer beauty. His muscles were incredible and it was obvious that he worked out in the G gym. He was not all bulked up like some competition body builders on earth get, but you could see all of his muscles and he did not have very much if any fat on him. Just enough to make his hard muscles soft to touch if he was not tensed up. His dick was a work of art. When soft, it was not much bigger than the average dick, but when he started getting hard, it was stunning. It took my breath away to look at him. Sure he was covered in hair, but he has none on his back and he had lots on his chest, but still he has some places where it was much thinner and you could see the trail of hair leading to his groin. I called this his happy trail leading to his happy place. The hair around his dick was long and rather straight. There was a slight curl, but not much. He also had some of the longest arm pit hair and it was dense and held his fragrance for me. I could live between his legs and under his arms and been happy for the rest of my life.

When I looked at his soft dick, I could see the head just barely poking out of the skin and there was lots of skin around the head. I could imagine me taking that skin and wrapping it around my body to keep warm if I was ever cold. His waist was small, very small and his legs and upper frame jutted out from this small waist. His upper body was almost like a triangle with his shoulders being wide and his body tapering on both sides to a very small waist. His upper thighs were massive when compared to mine, but they were proportional for his body. You could tell that he worked out on a cycling machine. We also had a vibrating machine to help counter the effects of reduced gravity and it tended to shake things up a bit. You could tell that he stood and worked out on the vibrator.

His nipples were amazing. They were not too big, but each nipple seemed to stand out about a cm, and they were just big enough that I loved to take them into my mouth and suck on them. First one and then the other found its way to my mouth to be sucked and carressed. Joel said that it felt good to him. He loved for me to suck on him and I did several times while we rested sometimes. The more I sucked on them, the bigger they seemed to get. One time he told me to suck on them, but not to move, because they were too sensitive. It seems that he was tripping on my nursing on his tits and he was getting physically too sensitive. That was all I needed to know and I sucked harder and then he came one time. Just looking at him made me want him in every way possible. I would have eaten him alive three times a day if it was possible. I get weak just thinking and writing about my mental picture of Joel.

We had showered before our duty stations, but neither of us took the time to shower before we met up here a few minutes ago. Therefore, we were not fresh and clean from a shower or the steam room, but were actually a few hours old from our showers. I could sense not a dirty stink odor, but not a pristine sterilized odor either. As Joel laid there next to me, I inhaled his fragrance and actually enjoyed the smell of a naked man in my arms more than ever before. He must have sensed that something was on my mind and he spoke to me.

"What are you doing?"

"I'm smelling you."

"Do I need to go shower."

"No. Please don't. I am enjoying the smell of you. You smell like a naked man. It's a good smell and makes me horny." I held him closer to me and lifted his arm and licked his pit and then kissed him. "Can you taste yourself. Does it make you as horny as it makes me?"

"Your mouth makes me horny. Your lips on mine make me horny. I want to spend all my off time with you and kissing you and feeling your body next to mine."

"And you want to fuck me again too, don't you."

"Well. Yes. If you will let me, I want to fuck you again. You are a good teacher. But I will let you fuck me as many times as you want to fuck me first. I love you and will do anything to please you. You know what power you have over me."

"I guess that you like the older man type. Hun."

"Only if they look like you and have that big fuck stick you keep referring to."

"You mean this little thing."

"It isn't so little."

"Not when going up your ass hole, but it sure is compared to yours."

"I can't help that. If I could I would have it cut down to size just so it would be the size you like. I would do it for you."

"That's not necessary. I like you being big. I just can't take it too often. I need a week to recover each time."

"A week." He looked disappointed.

"Well, maybe not that long." With that he ducked his head down and sucked my dick into his mouth. He sucked on me. I was hard before, but now I thought that it was so hard that it would break off if I hit it on anything. "You sure know how to get my interest."

"Just you lay back and relax and I want to give you pleasure." I laid back and he was getting real good at knowing what buttons on me to push.

"You are really ready to get your nut right now." I asked Joel.

"Get my nut?" I leaned up and reached down and gently grabbed his ball sack and moved around one of his balls.

"These are called your balls or your nuts. These are your family jewels. They are precious because they make your baby seeds and that is how you will have children, if any, in the future. When as the expression says get your nut, it means that you discharge the contents of your nuts. When you get your second nit, then it means that you climax again. In the old time it meant that you emptied first one nut and then the next one. Today we now know that that is not true. Each time you climax, you get a contribution from each nut." I enjoyed teaching him things about his body. He was so young and so beautiful in many ways. "I guess you are ready to fuck me now?" Boy did his eyes light up.

"If you want me to."

"I would rather be the first to get fucked right now, because that way you will cum much quicker than me and I won't have to let you fuck me for an hour or more. It is not that I don't want you to fuck me, but I am not certain that I can stand the pain for too long. I have to have more time to heal."

"I am so horny now. I don't know if I could last more than five minutes."

"That's even better. I enjoyed the long fucking you gave me earlier last time we were together, but I don't think my ass hole can last more than a few minutes right now without some major pain. I want to give you such pleasure as you have never before had, and I do so want to please you. But right now, I know I could not let you fuck me for too long with that mighty weapon you have between your legs." I reached over and got the tube of lubricant and applied it to him. I then spread my legs and opened them so he could crawl between them, face me, and hold me as he entered me. "Please go very slowly as I am still sore and you have not even touched me down there."

Joel bent over and applied his lips to my hole and kissed and tongued it and moved his tongue around my hole. His tongue was warm and moist and soothing to me. He stuck his tongue into me as far as he could go and played with my hole and licked me all over down there. He leaned up and then kissed me and whispered, "I love you more than life itself. You are letting me do this to you to please me. You don't know how happy this makes me." He kissed me some more, stuck his tongue in my mouth and turned his head sideways and covered my mouth with his. He tried to put my entire face in his mouth from the feelings of him all over my face and head. It felt good to be loved like this. He returned to my tender hole and again licked and tongued his way into me and then put some lubrication on his fingers. He put first one finger and then two inside of me. Finally he placed three fingers in me and I could feel my sensitive hole complaining. Then he placed his massive dick head at my rear entrance and gently pushed into me. I felt him enter me and the pain seared into me. However, once he was fully inside of me, I felt that same old familiar good kind of a hurt. He stayed perfectly still inside of me with his balls resting on my ass and his pubic hairs press up against my body. I hurt, but I also felt good to have him back inside of me. He was home.

"Go ahead. Fuck me you big mother fucker. Fuck me good, long and hard and then pump your nuts inside of me. I want you to pump me full of your love."

"Are you sure."

"Of course I am sure. I let you inside of me, didn't I. I want you to fuck me. You don't have to stretch it out more than you want, but I want you to enjoy yourself. I want you to completely enjoy yourself because I intend to fuck your ass so long and hard that you won't be able to sit down for a week. I also want to pump enough of my seed into you that your belly swells up and you have twins."

"But, I get to fuck you first."

"Yes. You are inside of me now. Remember this, I get to fuck you last. And I get to fuck you maybe two times after this before we go back on duty. I am trying to get you so sexed up that you cum in just minutes. Kiss me so I can spit into your mouth and let you taste me as you fuck my ass so that you will know that I intend to fuck you so hard you can't walk straight." Me talking dirty to him was having the desired effect. I could feel him swell inside of me and then he pulsed and pumped me full of his seed.

"I couldn't help it. You talking like that to me turned me on so much knowing that you wanted me and telling me all the things you were going to do to me, I couldn't help myself." He pulled out and bent over me. We kissed and then he looked hurt. Then he told me, "You are so sexy and turn me on so much. I hope I didn't hurt you. Are you mad that I came so quickly." I reached up and brought his face back to mine and kissed him again and slobbered all over his face.

"Of course not. I talked to you like that to get you all sexed up and wanting to cum so fast so I could give you pleasure before I had to ask you to pull out of me. I know you are so big, and I have not had the time to completely heal that I need before I can take you for such a long time again. I want to take you inside of my body when you want me, but I have to get used to you and to have time to heal between love makings. Then I can get used to taking you whenever you want me. I want to please you and push all your buttons and pull all your strings and turn you on like a firecracker."

"But you do. You do. And you did. I just couldn't last very long because you did all that to me by saying all those repulsive things about what you were going to do with me. It is just that to me doing them with you was not repulsive. I just don't ever want to disappoint you."

"You are so beautiful and you please me so much." I had to be careful. I was falling for this young man. What am I talking about, I had already fallen for this young stud. He wasn't exactly my ideal pick of beauty and perfection, but I found him so sexy and attractive, that I just couldn't help myself. I realized that I loved him. He made me so very happy. We lay there on the sleeping platform together. I held him as he lay there and held him to my chest. He fell into a deep sleep after we had sex and I let him sleep.

Chapter Eleven

Joel turned a little later. Now his back was toward me and my raging hard dick was pressed up against his back side. I continued to hold him. He woke up a few minutes later. He asked me, "Are you happy to hold me and feel me or is that just your foot pressing against me."

"Of course I am excited to hold you next to me."

"Well then why didn't you just put it inside of me."

"You were asleep."

"So. I would not have minded it. It's you. I am here with you, for you. You can put yourself inside of me any time you want to. If I am asleep, you don't even have to wake me up. But if I am about to cum, wake me up so I can enjoy it."

"You're kidding, right."

"I am kidding about waking me up before I cum, but I am here with you. Fuck me if you want to and you don't ever have to ask. I love you. I don't care what you do to me." I turned him and kissed him. I then lubricated myself and eased myself into him.

"Oh that feels so good and nice. I love having you inside of me. It is my favorite place for you to be."

We lay back down to rest and we fell asleep again. Within an hour I could feel him moving on my fuck stick and I was so hard I hurt. I reached around Joel and hugged him and chewed on his neck. He groaned and reached back and grabbed my ass and pulled me to him. He wanted me as far inside of him as possible. I held him to me and we fucked. He was in heaven and many times he told me so.

"Do it to me harder. Now deeper. Again and again. Pinch my tits and pound my ass hole. Keep doing it to me. I love to feel you inside of me. Do me, do me. Over and over again. Never stop and don't ever take it out of me." Then he would squeeze down on me and make me feel so good, and then he would relax and let me fuck him even harder and deeper. We fucked for a long time. He tensed up several times and each time I could feel him shake and move around underneath me. I know that he had several anal periods of intense pleasure, I call them anal orgasms. Each time I had my hand at the head of his dick and caught the clear fluid that oozed from him. I brought it up to my lips and then shared it with him. Over and over I pumped into him.

Finally I knew that I could not hold off any longer. I had slowed and stopped more than a dozen times to hold back, and then I stayed inside of him and lifted one of his legs and moved my upper body between his open legs and then moved him on to his back. A tricky maneuver performed on earth in one standard gravity. An easy maneuver if performed in the reduced gravity of space. I am now facing my lover with my dick fully up inside of his ass hole where it has been fucking away for the last hour. I lean over and take his huge dick in my mouth and suck on him and clean up the pool of his clear liquid on his stomach.

I lean over and chew on his tits, first one then the other. They are pert little things that just beg to be sucked and chewed. I loved them and wanted to suck on them for the rest of my life. Oh, my thoughts are giving me away. I leaned up and started chewing on his arm pits and inhaled his odor. What a powerful sexual turn on his pleasant body odor was to me. I bent over again and fucked hard and fast and sucked on him until he said he was cuming. I thought oh, how great. Cum you pretty boy, shoot your boy seeds into my mouth. Cum in my mouth and give me all your male essence for me to taste and swallow down. Thinking about this drove me on and I fucked even harder and tasted him when he shot into my mouth. Then I sent my male seed into his little boy rectum. I filled his little boy hole full of my seed and pumped into him over and over again. I liked to think of him as my little boy. Not a reference to his age or sex. Just my reference of complete adoring affection for him. My lover, my slightly younger bed partner.

I bent up and kissed him and shared his seeds with him. We slobbered all over each other and were both spent. We were completely and wonderfully spent. I laid back and gradually my member shrunk and came from inside of him. He reached for me and we held each other and kissed. We stayed like that locked in each other's embrace for a long, long time. We awoke later and had something to drink and eat and watched another movie while in each other's arms.

As we watched the movie together I reached down and held Joel with my free hand. I didn't play with him, but just held him. "Why are you doing that he finally asked?"

"Don't you enjoy it?"

"Of course I do."

"Well, I just enjoy holding on to that which belongs to me now." He smiled and looked up at me and kissed me.

"You don't know how happy that makes me to have you say that to me. I knew I felt that way about you, but I was not sure that you felt that way about me."

"Let me figure this one out from scratch, the beginning. I take your dick in my mouth, suck on you until you shoot your seed into my mouth and I swallow it down. I tell you how much I like it and the taste of you. I lick your ass hole and tell you how much I like the taste of it and you. I let you fuck me twice in just about as many days and it hurt like a mother fucker. And you ask me if I like you. And you doubt whether I love you. I just don't lick, tongue and kiss anyone's ass hole if I don't love them as much as life itself." His eyes swelled up and he smiled.

"I knew I loved you, but I wasn't sure you loved me."

"Well, you captured my heart and there is just not much I can do about it right now. I may have to space you to get over you."

"You wouldn't do that would you?"

"I guess if I did, I would have to go with you at the same time." He reached up and kissed me again and then held on to me between my legs. We watched the movie in that position, holding on to each other there between our legs. When I moved a little, he held me more closely.

"Mine. Mine. Mine, don't you dare move away so I can't hold on to what is mine." I loved this about him. He was young, and silly, and all mine. He was messing with my head and I just don't know if I was ever going to get over him. I also didn't know if I wanted to get over him. This is not at all what I intended. I just need to learn to keep my mouth shut. I was talking with my emotions and not my head. This was going where I wanted it to go, but I certainly had no intensions of it going in this direction. I don't know. I was confused about this. I just knew what I felt and, I had to stop telling Joel how I felt. This was not going at all how I intended it to be. I didn't want to love him, but I couldn't help it. I could not control my emotions when it came to Joel. Something was the matter with me.

When the movie was over, he turned to me and whispered in my ear. "Fuck me again my love and plant your love seeds inside of me and we will see if they can grow to be a baby for us to raise."

"You won't be disappointed if they don't grow will you."

"I will only be disappointed if you don't plant them and make it a good try just to see if they will grow inside of me."

"You know they won't."

"You know trying is just as much fun whether they grow or not. So shut up and fuck me for at least an hour and make it hurt."

"You really know how to make a guy feel welcome in your little hole. Well, if you want it to hurt, I can hit you in the head with my space boot."

"Only if your feet are in them and your legs are up over my head at the time. Then I can put my dick in you at the same time as you are hurting me and let you know what real pain feels like."

"You are a horny, insatiable fucker. My ass hole already has felt the pain of your third foot going up inside of it. That does make it hurt. But it is such a good hurt when you do it." I had to let Joel know that I loved him fucking me even if it did hurt. Then I thought I should not have disclosed the power he had over me. My emotions were taking over my mouth and saying the words that he could use to hurt or destroy me.

"Well, if my ass hole belongs to you, then yours belongs to me."

"I wish I could give it to you right now, it is so sore, I would gladly put my ass hole on you for the next few days until it heals."

"Here, let me kiss it and make it better." With that he raised my legs up and stuck his face in my ass crack again and ran his tongue over my puckered hole. It felt wonderful and soothed it again. He kept this up and I bent around and licked and tongued his hole that I had fucked not two hours ago. Our faces were buried in each other's ass holes and merrily licking, probing, and sucking away at the very most private parts of each other's bodies. Dicks are rather public as everyone can see your dick in the steam room and showers and elsewhere where men are naked in socially acceptable situations in small groups. Even in those groups, there is no sex or even the acceptance of any interest in sex with other men. However, most men never see the ass hole of another man let alone up close and personal. Personal enough to smell it, touch it, lick it, taste it and kiss it. Just the thought excited me when it belonged to Joel, and let me feel intimate with my lover. With the man that had captured my heart.

I suppose that if you are not attracted to the body of another man, large boy or whatever, you just can't explain it. The sheer happiness and pleasure to look at the naked or partially clothed body of a nice looking guy is indescribable. I guess that is why I never worried about if I was attracted to men. I just am. In the past I read that some people considered this attraction and choice of sexual partners a choice. Man, I had no choice in the matter. You know what turns you on.

Perhaps with enough conditioning you could learn to hate the feeling, but that is not going to make a naked woman look good and attractive to you. If so, then anyone could choose to only be attracted to women. I wish it worked that way. It just doesn't and there isn't anything anyone can do about it. You can't help how you feel, but you can help how you act. I can't help but to be attracted to other men. I just don't have to hump the ones that don't want to be humped (that's fucked in old slang or to have sexual intercourse with in our language.) You are who you are, so you might as well get used to it. You can't help whom you like sexually. I loved this little boy who had the plaything of a fully grown man. At 23 he was five years over the age of consent. I had been fucking my best friend since we were both about 16, so I knew what he knew. I knew that we both really liked it and sure as heck knew what we were doing to and with each other. We both loved it. We loved every centimeter of each other really.

Joel then spun around and positioned me to enter his hole while facing him. He was such a good looking young thing that this older man of 20 was again hard in an instant. I greased myself up and entered him. We fucked face to face. I loved the kissing, tongue play, face slobbering, ear biting, neck sucking and all the other things that went along with fucking face to face. I also loved to suck on his very big, as in jutting out, really big lip smacking tits. He had the most suckable tits I have ever seen on a man. I was like an insatiable nursing animal on them for him. He was loving the attention, and the incredible feelings it triggered through his body. I ate his arm pits and then chewed on them too. Several times underneath me he would tense up and I know that he was experiencing some type of intense pleasure period as I was fucking him. More than just the pleasure of getting fucked, but almost like an orgasm without cuming.

I had to slow down to rest and to vary my speed because I did not want to allow myself to cum just yet. I wanted to give my lover, there I was thinking in the wrong terms again, the most pleasure I could. When I knew I was getting close to that point of no return and my toes were tingling and my legs stiffening up and I was having a hard time concentrating, I leaned over and kissed him again. I know he knew I was close to cuming as he whispered into my ear, to bend down and suck him so he could piss into my mouth and I could drink it down as I was fucking him. That was all it took, I didn't have time to bend down, just the thought of what he wanted to do to me, sent me off the deep end. I thrust and rammed into his ass and came in great buckets.

"Tell me that you are going to spit into my mouth and get me all excited and then not keep your promises, I got you good. Maybe next time I will piss in your mouth and really set off your bells and whistles."

"And next time I would drink it down straight from the spout." I told him. I had to watch myself. I loved this boy. I knew that I wasn't prepared to do that, but I didn't have to tell him that. But just the thought of doing something that dirty and nasty with Joel made me cum while I was fucking him. I knew, but I didn't know if I was prepared to do that with Joel. At least, I did not think I was prepared to do that just yet. I know I had done it to him and he drank me down, but it was accidental on my part. I still was hesitant to drink him down that way. No, I knew that I never could.

We cuddled, spooned, kissed and held each other until it was just less than two hours from our shift. We got up and got dressed and then I left to go to my bunk and get my things and go to the G gym. I would do a light workout, take a steam bath and shower, and report for duty. I needed the rest of actually going to work to relax myself. I was sexually satisfied, but I needed some time away from someone who kept me fucking my brains out or vice versa, and where I couldn't get eight straight hours of sleep. These cat naps in between fucks were just not enough to let me recover completely. Getting your ass royally fucked, even if only for ten minutes wears a fellow out too.

Sex is great, but this was an example of too much of a good thing will kill you. That and getting run over on earth by a liquor delivery truck will do you in with some poetic justice. I know that is just about impossible with the latest anti crash devices that are now mandatory in all commercial vehicles, but you used to hear a lot about accidents before the devices were mandatory.

When I reported for duty, I worked on the training consoles learning to service them in a field situation. This is actually quite easy. All consoles are basically a computer with about ten different modules that you can change out. The real secret is to know how to get them in and out without breaking them, how to test to see if they are receiving power from the power module and if the power module is putting out the proper voltages and if the proper voltages are reaching the particular module. As to the module, you can't fix them. They are sealed against the vacuum of space and the extreme temperatures of space and the heat of use, so that they are not able to be serviced anywhere outside of the factory.

I had made friends with the man who serviced the modules at the space academy and he told me the factory didn't even repair them. Was not worth the effort, he said. They just destroyed them and sent you new ones. In the old days about 300 or 400 years ago they actually used wire and soldered connections to hook all this stuff all up. They soldered the connections inside of the modules and to interconnect the modules. Then they tried to use organic compounds to make the computer chips. Finally they were able to use light instead of electricity. Light travels at the same rate of speed as electricity, but the connections didn't get hot, the circuits didn't overheat and the entire thing could be sealed and was not subject to internal temperature changes. All connections were with fiber optics or their microfiber equivalent components.

This kept up the speed of signals traveling at the speed of light, with between one tenth and one hundredth the power consumption of soldered electrical connections, and essentially no heat when compared to electrically run components. So learning to repair the consoles was a breeze compared to what it would have been a few hundred years ago. Back then, it was a full time job and a career just learning to repair this stuff. What I learned in a few weeks of my spare time on the job would have taken me sometimes years of study and then I would only know a few systems. We had come a long way. Of course, 400 hundred years ago, they would have had me repairing actual circuit boards, checking for factory soldering errors and testing individual components. Now days a module may have 50 to 100 sub function components that I could test internally by switching the console to diagnostic mode and running a test automatically on each function unit, but not each part. It takes about four or five minutes to do this. Each functional component unit may have up to 10 billion individual components that are too small for the human eye to see in many cases, and certainly can not be fixed by me or anything short of the factory. Any one of those components may malfunction.

My main job is to find out which module is malfunctioning. I do try to locate the particular sub-function that is not working according to specifications so that I can report where the problem originates. This is purely so that we can tell the manufacturing team where we are having problems so they can correct the problems before they turn out another 5,000 defective units with potentially the same defect.

The officer of my watch summoned me after my watch to speak to him. He told me that my performance was satisfactory, but suggested that I not visit my girlfriend for at least another day or two. He saw my performance statistics and my performance was definitely down. Still within satisfactory levels, but down over my usual peak performance. I want to see you in your bunk asleep if I happen by and not out with the current woman of the month flavor who must be copulating your brains out for your performance to drop so suddenly from what appears to be a simple lack of sleep. I don't want to know her name and I don't care. But when you are finished with her you could tell me because the rest of the crew might want to renew acquaintances with her. I think she is keeping you happy and wearing you out at the same time. I thanked him and assured him that the relationship had been put on hold.

I went back to my bunk and Joel was already there fast asleep. I think we had both fucked our brains out and needed this rest. At the end of eight hours, I woke up refreshed and took care of personal business. Joel was still sleeping and I made sure not to wake him. I wandered back to the bunk area after three hours of eating, doing errands, getting cleaning dropped off, working out at the G gym with a steam room and various social visits to acquaintances, and other things. Joel was already up and about taking care of his business. I connected my personal pad to the desk station and sent messages to my parents, one to Tobert and asked how his love life was and read my mail and even read a message from John. He and his parents were now situated on the moon and he wanted me to come by and visit him. I was wondering how he was going to explain me to them. He couldn't really introduce me as the man he met and who fucked him all the way up the beanstalk. His parents were not stupid, and they surely might recognize me from the transport trip up the beanstalk. I had to be careful here. I wanted to fuck John again, but I also didn't want to hurt Joel's feelings. I really cared about Joel and as fine a piece of ass that John was, I was not giving up Joel to get John. On the other hand, I was not ready to give up John just yet.

With John, there did not seem to be a future right now. Joel and I could settle down onboard ship and work here and live together as a couple for the next three or four decades if we wanted. I could also do my year's internship and go back to earth and finish up with a specialization. The corps would see to it that Joel received an earthside assignment or could continue in school on Earth. In another year or two with good ratings onboard my ship, I could be a ship's navigator, copilot or even one day a captain. The salary was good, not that I needed the money, but the benefits were great. I could bring my spouse of either sex with me. We would be given an allowance and special berthing accommodations for being married. The service was the one place where they did not discriminate against M-M couples. They even encouraged them because there were no children usually, and that was just another added expense for the service to provide for and maintain. Joel was good at his job and he didn't need me to provide for him, but being married to a senior ship's officer would not hurt his career. If I rose in the ranks, he would always be assigned to my ship and go as far as his own talents would take him.

On the other hand, I did not know anything about John except that he was stunning looking, as was Joel, and had such a nice cute pert fuckable ass hole, while on the other hand, so did Joel. Heck, I really didn't see any way around this dilemma. I might just have to marry both of them, at the same time. Something I knew was not legally possible. Then I wondered if I could leave Gert out of this three or what was now becoming a four cornered relationship. My only hope is that I made up my mind before any of them found out about the other. To tell you the truth, I don't know who would win right now. No matter how I decided, I would be a winner with any one of them.

I know that I could not have more than one husband. I don't think I could handle more than one, but I can dream, can't I.

On some off worlds, a man could have more than one wife for the purpose of populating the world, but while the law applied to M-M couples, it was rarely used as men tend to be more jealous than a woman when there are not enough men to go around. Once a week for some women was more than enough after two kids and all that housework. Besides, I am sure that any one of these fine masculine specimens could find anyone they wanted given a little of time and testicles big enough to force them to actually go out there and seek companionship. I found John. However, Gert and Joel and I each found each other. The longer someone is looking the easier it is to get up the courage.

I found out that Joel had also dropped in his performance tests and was told to cut back to two women on each of his off shift periods by his supervisor. I questioned him if he thought his supervisor knew about us. His response was that he didn't think so because he encouraged Joel to use that big thing he had seen between his legs in the G gym and to tell him which philly he was breeding so that when Joel got finished with her, she might be ready for a rest with a guy of more normal proportions like himself. I had to promise to double date with him some time to introduce him to her. I asked if he was serious. I don't think so, he responded as I happen to know he is married and his wife works in Astrogation and is quite a good looking woman. We were saved again by his quick thinking. I was constantly impressed by Joel the more I got to know him and the way he functioned. I also liked the way he fucked, but I could not let him know that. I forgot. I already had told him I loved his big dick inside of me. Well, the best laid plans of mice and men department took over there. He told me that his supervisor isn't a bad looking man, but I think you are better looking, and I am not about to share you with anyone.

I would just have to worry about this problem another day.

About the Author

The author was born in the northern part of the United States. Fleeing from the snow, ice and cold weather, he eventually moved to warmer climates. He was educated in both the scientific and legal fields and received several degrees in those endeavors. He had lived practically half of his life as a student before actually going to work for a living. He worked diligently and productively for many years. In his late 50's his health took a sudden turn in an unexpected direction for the worse. He was forced to retire, but believed that he still had an active mind. He now writes technical articles and publications in his academic fields. However, believing that everyone has to have a hobby, he has turned some of his bad intentions to writing adult novels. The author now lives with his two furry, four legged dependents who constantly guard him and limit his writing activities. He hopes you have as much enjoyment in reading this story as he in writing it for you. 9.21.48